By SCOTTY CADE

Acting Out
Before the Final Encore • Final Encore
The Mystery of Ruby Lode
The Royal Street Heist
Sunrise Over Savannah • Chasing the Horizon
An Unconventional Courtship • An Unconventional Union

LOVE SERIES
Wings of Love
Bounty of Love
Treasure of Love
With Z.B. Marshall: Foundation of Love

Published by DREAMSPINNER PRESS
http://www.dreamspinnerpress.com

FINAL ENCORE

Scotty Cade

Published by
Dreamspinner Press

5032 Capital Circle SW, Suite 2, PMB# 279, Tallahassee, FL 32305-7886 USA
http://www.dreamspinnerpress.com/

ISBN: 978-1-63476-117-8
Digital ISBN: 978-1-63476-118-5
Library of Congress Control Number: 2014922790
Second Edition March 2015
First Edition published by Dreamspinner Press, November 2010.

Printed in the United States of America

This paper meets the requirements of
ANSI/NISO Z39.48-1992 (Permanence of Paper).

To Kell, my partner and best friend of eighteen years, who suffered through many long days and nights alone in front of the television while I wrote this book. Thank you, thank you. Your continuing love, support, and encouragement make me who I am today. I love you.

To my best girlfriend, Mary (Peg) Plumstead, who grew to love these characters as much as I did, and who always encouraged and challenged me to go well beyond my capabilities. Your natural instinct and ability to look beyond what you were reading, along with your incredible creative skills, saved me too many times to count. You're the best.

And finally, last but certainly not least, to my friend and editor Andi Byassee. Trust me when I tell you, you're a godsend! You take all my misspelled words, bad punctuation, and run-on sentences and turn them into stories. You work your magic and voilà. A novel! Thank you from the bottom of my heart.

Chapter One

BILLY EAGAN left New Orleans for Nashville with a few thousand dollars in his pocket—and a dream.

Born and raised in the Big Easy, Billy was the first in his family to leave the city, and his loved ones, behind. New Orleans is a town rich in history and tradition; she forces you to love her, and most never leave her embrace, but Billy had bigger-than-average dreams, and he wasn't about to stay put and live the simple life, no matter how much he loved his family and his home.

His middle-class upbringing had taught him his strong work ethic, but his parents had taught him to dream, dream big, and never give up on those dreams.

On the morning he left, his entire family was there to send him off. He started his truck and rolled down the window for a final good-bye. His mother kissed him, and his father shook his hand and said, "I'm proud of you, son. You're leaving everything you know behind and making a new life for yourself, and that takes real guts."

As he pulled out of the driveway, Billy thought back to the many things he'd done over the years to make his father say those words. How strange that leaving his family behind to pursue his aspirations would be the thing that made his father the most proud.

He left with a sense of comfort and pride that warmed him to his core.

Billy had to concentrate on his driving while he navigated through the city, but once he reached the interstate, he relaxed into the journey. He turned on the radio, and the first thing he heard was

Percy Sledge singing "When a Man Loves a Woman." And didn't that bring back memories?

His mamma was the one who taught him to love music. She had a beautiful voice, and he always felt a little sad thinking how she might have had a singing career if she hadn't stayed at home to raise Billy and his sisters.

Before school put an end to his days at home with his mother, he used to "help" her with the housework. Vacuuming was his favorite. He remembered riding on the canister of the Hoover singing along with his mamma to the very song playing on the radio now.

And here he was, on his way to Nashville, Tennessee, to take a shot at stardom. Did he have what it took? He figured he'd find out soon enough.

Billy's drive from New Orleans to Nashville was long and mostly uneventful. The uninterrupted hours on the highway were marked with country radio stations fading in and out. It tickled his fancy to think of them as stepping-stones to his future.

By the time he reached the outskirts of the city, Billy was tired. The malls, business parks, and factories he passed looked much like they did anywhere. Then, suddenly, the highway took a jog and a little rise, and there it was. Nashville. Music City. The heart of the country-music industry, Music Row, was not visible from this distance, of course, but Billy recognized the famous "Batman building," the AT&T building that dominated the city skyline. His heart gave a little lurch.

This is for real. I'm really here. Look out, Nashville, here I come.

Billy's first order of business was finding a place to stay, temporarily at least. He'd saved up a little money—not a lot, but enough to keep him fed and sheltered for a while. Hopefully, he'd find a job quickly and maybe rent a room or a cheap apartment somewhere. Meanwhile, a motel seemed like the best option, and he found a Motel 6 just off the interstate and only ten minutes or so from downtown. The price was right and the room was cheap, if nothing special. If the sheets were a little coarse, he was too tired to notice.

The next morning he made his way to the Cracker Barrel next to the motel for breakfast, and while he was there, he studied the want ads in the *Nashville Tennessean* and circled a few likely prospects. Luckily, Billy had some marketable skills. He'd done some construction work in NOLA and had been manager of the lumber section of a big building supply store. But what he had loved the most—other than singing, of course—was the time he'd spent with his dad raising quarter horses. He shared his dad's passion for the loveable beasts, and they'd had some good times together riding and caring for the animals. Still, Billy didn't think it very likely he'd find a job demanding that sort of experience. Beggars couldn't be choosers. When he got back to his room, he started making calls.

That day set his routine for his first week in Nashville. Meals at Cracker Barrel, studying want ads, calling prospective employers. He allowed himself a little time each day to drive downtown and get to know his way around the city, especially that magical area around 16th and 17th Avenues South known as Music Row. When the inevitable homesickness set in during those first lonely days, the siren call of Music Row helped him keep his spirits up and cling to his determination. He missed his family terribly, but he never once thought about turning around. He was going to give this new journey everything he had.

Near the end of that first week, he got a call from an ad he'd answered. It turned out his experience with horses might be what would get him a job after all. The position was for a foreman at a large horse farm that boarded horses as well as specializing in guided rides for tourists—the Lazy H Ranch in Mount Juliet, Tennessee, just outside of Nashville. After a brief conversation, he agreed to meet the owner at ten o'clock the next morning. It wasn't singing, but he felt lucky to have the opportunity, and it would pay the bills until—until, he told himself, not when—he found something in the music business.

Chapter Two

BILLY TURNED in under the large steel arch with The Lazy H Ranch etched on it and looked down at his watch to confirm the time. *Nine forty-five. Right on time.*

He cautiously drove down a dust-covered road, with lush pastures on either side. After a half mile or so, the road ended at a farmhouse flanked by two large barns. When he got out of his truck, he was examined, rather than greeted, by a rough and unfriendly looking man. He was short and stocky, his frame overburdened with at least thirty extra pounds. His skin was scarred from years of acne and his teeth were stained from what appeared to be chewing tobacco—as indicated by the Styrofoam cup he spat into as he studied Billy. Hoping this wasn't the owner, Billy introduced himself and then sighed with relief when he learned the man was a ranch hand named Buck Stevens.

"You can wait near the east barn," Buck said, gesturing over his shoulder. "And someone'll be with you shortly."

Billy waited around for about forty-five minutes, but no one approached him. He was about to go after Buck to remind him he was still waiting when he saw a tall, ruggedly handsome man walking in his direction. The man, who reminded him of an older version of the Marlboro Man from the old cigarette commercials, walked up and offered his hand.

"Hi, I'm Jules James. I'm the owner of the ranch. Are you William Eagan, by any chance?"

"Yes, sir, but I go by Billy."

They shook hands and looked each other over for a few seconds before Jules broke the silence. "I had just about given up on you, son. I thought your interview was at ten o'clock."

"It was, sir," Billy replied. "I arrived at nine forty-five, and Buck told me to wait at the east barn and someone would find me. I was just about to go look for Buck when I saw you walking over."

"That's funny," Jules said. "I told Buck to have you meet me at the west barn. I have a mare about to foal, and I want to be there in case there are any problems."

"I'm sorry about the confusion, sir," Billy said. "Would you like me to come back?"

Jules shook his head. "No. I've got some time. Why don't you walk with me to the west barn, and we can have a chat along the way."

"Yes, sir," Billy said.

On the short walk, Billy filled Jules in on his extensive experience with horses and explained why he was in Nashville. Billy felt certain Jules had heard the same story many times before, but to his credit, he listened intently and even offered a few words of encouragement.

They soon reached the stall housing the expectant mare. She was lying on her side, and Billy observed her tense up every few minutes with contractions. It was apparent to him she still had some time before she'd deliver, but he thought she looked a bit distressed. He decided to hold his tongue until he could get a better gauge on the situation.

Together, they entered the stall and examined the mare closely as Jules continued to tell Billy about the ranch operations and the job he had available. After the examination was complete, Billy was sure something was wrong.

"I'm pretty sure the foal is breached," Billy said hesitantly.

Jules smiled weakly. "Good call," he said, pulling off a rubber glove. "I was just about to tell you the same thing."

Billy spent the next several hours helping Jules try to get the foal positioned properly for a natural birth, and eventually they succeeded. By late afternoon the little filly was born healthier than either expected. With the danger now behind them, Jules and Billy cleaned up and headed back to the tack room to put the supplies away. As they entered the small enclosure, Buck was filling up the feed barrels. He looked up and eyed Billy warily.

"Well, Billy," Jules said, "I'm pretty impressed with your knowledge and skill. As far as I'm concerned, I've seen as much as I need to see. If you want the job, it's yours."

Before Billy could speak, Buck turned around with a disgruntled look on his face and stormed out of the tack room, brushing Billy's shoulder roughly in the process.

"Wow," Billy said. "What was that all about?"

"Oh, don't pay him any mind," Jules replied. "He wants the job, but I just don't think he has the skills to be a foreman. He's a little hotheaded for my taste."

Billy sighed. "If I take the job, is he going to be a problem for me?"

"Don't you worry, I'll deal with him," Jules said. "Does this mean I have a new employee?"

Billy held out his hand. "Yes, sir," he replied, and Jules sealed the deal with a handshake.

"My wife and I own a little club on Broadway," Jules said on the way back to the farmhouse. "I'm headed there for a couple of beers, then right back here to check on our little one. You want to join me?"

"Sure. Why not?"

When Jules's truck pulled up to Jean's Magnolia Saloon, Billy remembered Jules's words and chuckled to himself. *This is no little club.* The two men got out and headed inside.

Jules opened the door to the dimly lit lounge, and Billy's vision took a few seconds to adjust. He glanced around the saloon, which was even larger than it looked from the street, about the size of a small supermarket.

On one side, a large mahogany bar ran the full length of the room. Opposite the bar was a raised stage with a colorful set of drums, an electric keyboard, and various other musical instruments on stands. An expansive oblong dance floor—surrounded by split-rail fencing with openings at each end and dusted with what looked and smelled like fresh sawdust—held place in the center of the room. Overstuffed chairs in numerous groupings, along with high cocktail tables and barstools, provided ample and comfortable seating and finished off the look.

Jules led Billy to the bar and introduced him to a beautiful, well-dressed, gracefully maturing woman behind the counter, pouring beer from a tap. His first thought was that she must be Jules's wife. And his second thought was that she didn't look like she belonged behind a bar. She was tall and slender, about five foot nine and a hundred and twenty-five pounds, give or take. She had dark brown hair, deep brown eyes, and appeared to be the epitome of joy, strength, and sincerity. Her smile was beaming.

Billy had heard the term "ageless" before but had never really understood it. It had nothing to do with how young a person looked, although this woman looked quite youthful. It was really about natural style and confidence.

"Hey, hon," Jules said. "This is Billy Eagan. He just joined the Lazy H as our new foreman, but he really wants to be a country singer." He winked. "Billy, this is my wife, Jean."

"Pleased to meet you, Mrs. James," Billy said removing his hat and offering his hand.

"Nice to meet you too, Billy," she replied as they shook hands. "Welcome to my saloon, and please call me Jean. You any good, by the way?"

Billy chose his words carefully, not wanting to sound conceited. "Well, ma'am—" He hesitated. "—I've been told I am by more than just my family and friends, and I sure hope no one's been pulling my leg."

"Have you been performing for a long time?" Jean asked.

"Since I was a thirteen, ma'am," Billy replied. "I started out in my school's musical theater group, and I've been singing ever since."

Jean looked surprised. "Musical theater, huh?" she asked with an intrigued tone in her voice. "How did you end up in country music?"

7

"In my senior year of high school I taught myself to play guitar and discovered country music. I fell instantly in love with it, formed a band, and it all took off from there."

"I see," Jean said through a warm smile. "Well, Monday nights once a month we have an open mic competition, and you're surely welcome to join us. Many celebrities got their start here. We have a crowd of talent scouts that hang around on a regular basis to see if they might just catch the next big thing."

"When's the next one?" Billy asked.

"Monday night," Jean said.

"Day after tomorrow?" Billy asked.

Jean nodded. "But you better show up early because every newcomer dreaming of stardom will be here and itching for a spot on that stage, and we only have time for ten acts before the headliner starts."

"Yes, ma'am," Billy said, nodding his head.

"And the best thing is," she added, "if you win, you get to be the opening act for the entire month until the next open mic night."

"Seriously?" Billy asked.

Jean nodded. "We open the mic at ten, but you should plan to get here by eight to sign up."

Jean turned when someone down the bar called her name. "I hope to see you Monday night," she added before she headed down the bar.

"I'll be here," Billy assured her as she walked away. "And thanks."

Jules and Billy sat at the bar enjoying small talk for an hour or so, getting to know one another at a leisurely pace. Jean came and went as business dictated but always joined the conversation when she could. Finally, after the relief bartender showed up, she landed on the barstool next to Billy. "So what's the hot topic you two seem to be so involved in?" she asked.

"Oh, we were talking about the ranch," Billy said, turning slightly in her direction but not excluding Jules. "Your husband was telling me you guys live in Lebanon, but that he sometimes stays at the ranch when he needs to pull a double, or when they're expecting a foal—things like that."

"That's my Jules all right," Jean said, leaning around Billy to Jules, offering him a warm smile.

They seem so in sync, Billy thought.

"So how long have you two been married?" he asked curiously.

"Forty-nine years now and still going strong," Jules said as he reached behind Billy and gave Jean a squeeze. "What about you? Do you have a girlfriend, son?"

"Uh, no, sir," he replied.

Jean chimed in, "I don't mean to assume anything, but do you have a boyfriend?"

"Uh… not at the moment, ma'am," Billy said, unable to hide his surprise.

Both Jules and Jean smiled, and Billy's cheeks warmed. "If you don't mind me asking," Billy inquired, "how did you know about me? I mean, I try not to spit sequins when I talk."

Jules and Jean chuckled. "Relax," Jean said. "Our son is gay, and we've been around you sweet boys for over twenty years now. One's gaydar becomes pretty accurate after so many years."

"I guess it would," Billy agreed. "So, Jules? How will the boys back at the ranch react when they find out?"

"Oh hell," Jules said. "No need to worry about those lugs. They're all harmless. You may take a little ribbing every now and again, but if you pull your weight they'll respect you and it won't matter none. But…," he added, "I would keep my eye on Buck. As I mentioned, he's somewhat hotheaded, and he already has a chip on his shoulder since he thinks you stole his job."

Billy nodded. "I can take care of myself in that department. But just for safety's sake, when Buck's around I'll sleep with one eye open and a baseball bat under my bed."

"I don't think it will come to that," Jules said. "But I think it's a good idea just the same."

A couple of hours later, Jules stood and looked at Jean. "I don't know about you, honey, but I'm beat."

"So am I," she agreed. "Too bad you have to go all the way back to the ranch."

Billy stood. "I can drive your truck back to the ranch and check on the little filly," he offered. "I mean, if you're comfortable with that."

Jules looked at Jean, and they both nodded. "That would be very much appreciated. Just call me if anything looks or feels out of place as far as the filly's concerned. You have my number."

"Do you need me to pick you up in the morning?" Billy asked.

"Nope," Jean said. "I have an early appointment, so I'll drop him off on my way into town."

Billy drove back at a leisurely pace, enjoying a mental recap of all that had happened to him since he'd left New Orleans. He eventually made it back to the ranch and, after checking on the mare and filly, hopped into his truck and headed back to his motel room for the last time. His new job came with lodgings at the ranch, which would really help with expenses. When he finally arrived, he stripped down to his shorts, brushed his teeth, and climbed into bed. For a long while, he lay there and anticipated the next day—and Monday night.

JUST AFTER sunrise the next morning, Billy drove out to the ranch. It was Sunday, so things were a little quieter than they would be normally, but when there are animals to care for, every day is a workday. He completed the necessary paperwork for new employees and was given a slip of paper that assigned him to the Palomino bunkhouse, with a highlighted map directing him to his new home. He followed the directions to a large, rustic log cabin. He pushed the screen door open and entered hesitantly.

The main room contained six bunk beds on each side, the bunks numbered one through twelve. Between each bed were double locker-like closets and two small footlockers, all with corresponding numbers. A small kitchen area and a set of doors he assumed were the entrances to the bathrooms and showers took up the back of the room.

Several men Billy figured were other ranch hands sat at a small table in the kitchen, along with Buck Stevens. Billy introduced himself and nodded in Buck's direction. After chatting with the men, he found out that many of them were also looking for their chance at success. Some of these guys had been trying to break into the business for many years, and some, like him, had just started their journey. Buck said he wasn't a singer but claimed his girlfriend was a major up-and-coming star. Most of the guys rolled their eyes and smirked.

The older, more experienced guys seemed worn-down and weary, while the newcomers had a gleam in their eyes he'd bet was in his as well. He couldn't decide whether he was encouraged or disheartened by his fellow dreamers. Nashville was full of talented, aspiring entertainers and only the best of the best would make it.

Will I be one of the best? Billy mused as he found his bunk and unpacked what little he had brought with him.

One of the hands told Billy he should report to Jules at the west barn. When he arrived there, he found Jules on his knees, visiting with the newest addition to the ranch.

"Morning," he said. "How's our little girl doing?"

"Just fine," Jules said looking up at him. "Partly thanks to you."

"Doing my job is all," Billy said.

"You weren't hired yet then, son," Jules teased.

Billy smiled. "I guess you got me there."

Jules got to his feet, patted the filly gently, and reassured the mare with a generous head rub before he left the stall.

"So," Jules started, "as I mentioned yesterday, you'll be the foreman in charge of the ranch hands who care for the boarded horses and host the trail rides for the tourists."

Billy nodded, recalling what Jules had explained to him the day before. Each day ranch hands acting as tour guides lead groups of riders on a breathtaking five-hour tour of Mount Juliet, known as the city between the lakes. Midway through the ride, each guide would set up a picnic lunch and then return with his group by three in the afternoon.

"I'll probably lead a tour tomorrow to demonstrate how I want them to go and how and where I like the lunch presented, but because you'll have six groups to supervise each day, I think it would be wise for you to get to know the guides by accompanying each of them as well. Both to familiarize yourself with the terrain and with the guides and their capabilities."

"Agreed," Billy said.

"Now, each morning there are up to thirty-six horses to saddle and prepare. You and your staff arrive sharply at seven o'clock, and your day will be done no later than five thirty."

"That's great," Billy said. "This schedule will give me plenty of time for a quick nap, a shower, and some dinner before I hit the town in search of a gig."

"Figured as much," Jules said. "So there you have it, son. Take your first day as it comes, hanging around the barn and observing, and tomorrow you can start joining the guides."

"Yes, sir," Billy said. "And thanks again for the opportunity."

"My pleasure, son. I'll catch up with you later."

"Yes, sir."

As instructed, Billy stayed around the barn and helped the guides saddle their horses to get familiar with the tack, the horses, and their personalities. When the day was done, he remained behind to make sure the tack room was set up to his liking. He wanted to see how much pride and care the guides took in their work. When he finally retired, it was nine o'clock, and he was exhausted. He grabbed a quick sandwich from the mess hall and made his way back to his bunkhouse, showered, and went straight to bed.

Before the first rays of sunshine peeked through the window shades, and before any of the other hands were even stirring, Billy was up and ready to go. He found his way around the small kitchen and made the first pot of coffee. When the pot finished brewing, he poured himself a cup and headed to the west barn.

Once again Jules had beaten him to the punch.

Gonna have to get up a lot earlier if I'm ever going to beat him in, Billy thought.

"Morning, son," Jules said. "Sleep okay?"

Billy smiled broadly. "Hardly slept at all. Guess I'm just too excited about today and… tonight. I'll be just fine, though. Where do you want me to start?"

"Well, I was gonna have you start in the tack room, but it appears you already *tack*led that area," Jules said humorously.

Billy laughed at the play on words. "Yes, sir. Last night."

After observing his first day, Billy knew that every bridle, saddle, and blanket was personalized with the horse's name on it, so he wanted it all sorted as such. He had spent a couple of hours organizing everything the way he expected it to be and would show each hand the next morning how he wanted to find the room at the end of each day.

"Nice job with that, Billy," Jules said. "Since the other hands won't get here for another hour or so, maybe you can set up each saddling station, just to get used to the process."

"On it, sir."

"By the way, we have only eight riders in each group today, so it should be a fairly light day."

"Yes, sir."

"Billy, I'm really impressed. If you're as good onstage as you are here, Jean might just have another star on her hands."

Billy felt an overwhelming sense of pride. "Thank you, sir. I do my best."

"And stop calling me sir!"

"Yes, sir—I mean, Jules."

Jules laughed heartily. "That's better. Now let's get a move on. Day's a-burnin'."

Billy accompanied Jules, who led one of the tours as planned, and it all went very well. Billy truly enjoyed the countryside, stunning with summit, valley, and lake views. They stopped for lunch at one of the many picnic areas available along the trails, and Billy paid special attention to how Jules wanted everything done.

When the tour was over, Billy helped the guides remove the saddles and blankets, replace the bridles with halters, and take the horses one by one to the automatic walker for a cooldown period. After they were adequately cooled, the ranch hands released them in the pasture to graze until it was time to put them in their stalls, feed them, and secure them for the evening. The day went by very fast and without a hitch. By five o'clock Billy was headed to the bunkhouse to get ready for his big night.

When he arrived some of the other ranch hands, already off duty, were sitting around a large table on the porch, having a beer and waiting for dinner. They kindly invited Billy to join in, and he obliged. The first thing several of them wanted to know was if Billy could cook. One night a week, the mess hall was closed, and the hands shared cooking responsibilities in rotation. They were wondering what kind of grub they could expect when it rolled around to Billy's turn. Billy assured them he knew his way around a kitchen, and they seemed relieved and pleased.

In the short time he had, Billy felt pretty comfortable around them. Much to his surprise, someone brought up Buck's name, and they all had a little to say about the guy. The general consensus was that he was not well liked.

Everyone agreed he was very rough around the edges. He pushed his girlfriend too hard and used her as his meal ticket, although they all agreed she wasn't nearly good enough to make it in the business. After about an hour, Billy excused himself and explained that he was headed to Jean's for open mic night. They all wished him well and said to give Jean their best. A couple of the guys even said they would be there to lend some support. He thought they were probably more curious than anything else, but he knew a familiar face would make him feel a little more at ease.

Billy showered quickly and dried off. He towel dried his thick black hair and then wrapped the towel around his waist and headed back to his bunk to dress. He put on his best pair of black Wranglers, an emerald green silk shirt, his favorite black boots, and his lucky black belt with a large, oval-shaped silver buckle he'd won at a rodeo back in New Orleans.

When he finished dressing, he reached up to the top of his locker and pulled down a box containing his black Stetson with his favorite onyx and rhinestone hatband. He stuck it on his head, stepped back, and opened the locker door. Looking at himself in the mirror, he thought, *This is as good as it's gonna get.*

Chapter Three

AFTER PICKING up a burger and a Coke at a drive-through and eating it on the way, Billy pulled into the parking lot at Jean's at exactly seven forty-five. He checked his teeth for burger residue in the rearview mirror, got out of his truck, and nervously started for the entrance.

He was surprised to see the place was already very busy. Scanning the club, he saw Jules sitting at the far end of the bar talking to Jean, and he walked over. "Evening, folks."

Jules smiled genuinely. "Hey, son."

"Hey, honey," Jean said, giving him a kiss on the cheek.

"You ready for tonight?" Jules asked.

"Oh yeah, I'm ready. Chomping at the bit, so to speak."

Jean handed him a clipboard containing a sign-up sheet and a list of cover songs made popular by other artists.

"You better sign up and pick out your song choices so I can pass them along to the house band. You'll need to pick two because if you're chosen by the crowd as one of the top three performers, you'll do a second song."

Before he chose his songs, Billy took a quick scan of the bar to see who his audience was. To his surprise he saw Buck Stevens sitting with his arm around a fairly attractive older woman with auburn hair in a really big hairdo. *That must be the meal ticket the guys were referring to. But who wears their hair like that anymore?*

Turning his attention back to the audience, Billy saw it consisted mostly of women. He thought because of that he should choose an especially tender song to try to establish an immediate connection with the ladies.

He quickly signed his name on the clipboard and reviewed the song list. After much thought, for his first song he chose "Moments" by Emerson Drive and for his second song, if he needed it, he chose "Love Me If You Can" by Toby Keith.

With that done, he decided to have a beer while he waited for the show to start. Just as the bartender brought his drink, Jules came over and sat on the empty barstool next to him.

"Nervous, son?"

"Not a chance, sir. I was born to do this."

They sat at the bar and talked until the lights dimmed and the house band took the stage promptly at ten o'clock.

Jean walked up onstage and welcomed everyone to the saloon and to open mic night. Shortly after she introduced the first act, Billy started to get butterflies. Not because he didn't think he was good enough to compete, but because the first performer was having some difficulty keeping up with the band. Eventually the band followed her pace, and things improved. But he hadn't sung with this band before either, and that could prove to be a challenge.

Billy decided he would stick with the original artist's version of the song and not do any runs or ad-libbing. He wondered how many of the other performers had already sung with the band at previous open mic nights. That could give them a slight edge. His mind was starting to get the best of him, so he forced himself to calm down and focus on the other performers instead.

Before he knew it, he was next. Jean took the stage again. "Ladies and gentlemen. For the first time at Jean's, please welcome Mr. Billy Eagan."

He had time for one last thought. *I'm about to take the stage at Jean's Magnolia Saloon.*

Billy walked onto the stage, retrieved a barstool from the back corner, moved it to center stage, took a seat, and adjusted the microphone stand. He nodded to the band as a signal that he was ready. As the band played the intro, he waited, and then he began to sing.

The song was about a down-and-out man attempting suicide by jumping off a bridge and being rescued by a homeless person. He knew the song would touch some hearts. It had great range, a good story, and more importantly, something people could identify with. It wasn't an upbeat song, but it showed off his vocal range, and besides, all of the performers before him had done songs like Garth Brooks's "Friends in Low Places" and George Strait's "They Call Me the Fireman," as if it were karaoke night at the local bowling alley. This was his chance to stand out. It was a make-it-or-break-it song. As he reached the first chorus, he looked around the room and knew in his heart he had captured everyone's attention. From that point he no longer second-guessed his song choice; he just sang.

When he finished, the audience jumped to their feet and filled the room with applause. Billy was blown away and didn't quite know what to do. As he looked over at the bar, he saw Jules and Jean, eyes wide with amazement and clapping like there was no tomorrow.

As Billy exited the stage and made room for the next performer, the crowd yelled for more. Billy flashed his biggest smile, removed his hat, bowed at the waist, and walked offstage. *I hope I'll have another chance to sing for you later.*

Billy nervously headed over to join Jules and Jean at the bar. *God, I hope they liked me.*

When he reached the bar he received a big hug from Jean. "No one was pulling your leg, honey," she said. "Great job!"

He also got a warm handshake and accolades from Jules, as well as a few people standing at the bar.

He ordered a beer, took a seat, and calmly watched the rest of the performers, sizing up his competition. When just about everyone had sung, he went over all the acts in his head. In his opinion there were only a couple as good as or better than he was. The first was an attractive dark-haired lady named Melanie Dodge. Melanie had a Gretchen Wilson look and a similar sound as well. He thought she would be tough to beat. The other contender was a short redheaded guy named Greg Ryan, whom he dubbed Opie because he reminded Billy of Opie Taylor, the little boy Ron Howard played on *The Andy Griffith Show*. His size and looks were deceptive because when he opened his mouth to sing, out came a deep, sweet, soulful sound that was as good as Billy's, if not better. As he continued to study his rivals, the sound of applause snapped him out of his concentration.

Jules leaned over and said, "Just one more act to go, son, and we've heard her before. She's... well... I'll let you judge for yourself."

The last performer was Buck's girlfriend, who wore a shiny gold outfit that accentuated her shapely figure.

However old she is, she's in great shape.

Jean walked onstage and stood in front of the microphone again. "One more entertainer to go," she said. "I'm sure you all recognize this little lady. Please welcome back to the stage Ms. Tina Roth."

As the intro to her song began, Billy knew immediately that she was singing Tammy Wynette's "Stand By Your Man." He got to his feet, worried, knowing how difficult it was to tackle a Tammy Wynette tune unless you were a superstar. Billy looked around, blushed as if everyone could read his mind, and secretly thought, *Man, I hope she can't sing.*

As soon as Tina opened her mouth and busted out the first line about how hard it was to be a "wo-man," Billy sat back down. Tina's voice was somewhere between a twang and a howl, and in his opinion, she should never have attempted such an iconic number.

Jules looked at him with an "I told you so" smile, and Billy sighed in relief. He felt fairly certain then that he'd made the top three.

Tina finished and everyone clapped politely. Buck whistled while she took her bow. All that remained was to determine the top three.

As Jean took the stage once again, she asked all the performers to join her. One by one, they walked up and fell in line. She called their names, and each one stepped forward. By a round of applause, the audience voted for their favorites. The winners of round one would get to do a second song, and one of them would ultimately win the competition.

Just as Billy had previously thought, both Melanie and Greg received thunderous rounds of applause when their names were called. Now there were only four of them left. The next two performers received polite but minimal applause, and then Billy heard his name.

He stepped forward and received the same thunderous applause as Melanie and Greg, plus a bonus in the form of a few ladies jumping up and down in the front row. Needless to say, he was happy with the outcome. Only one more to go, and it was Buck's girlfriend, so he thought he had a pretty good chance. She received the same polite applause as the two acts before him, and just like that, he was in round two. He couldn't have been happier.

As Tina walked off the stage, he saw Buck grab her by the arm and lead her to the restroom area. Billy could hear Buck's raised voice over the very loud sounds of the club, and he suddenly felt sorry for her.

Billy made his way back to the bar and ordered another beer. He bought a round for Jules and Jean when they showed up, and they all listened as the house band played a set before the final three performers did their last songs. The two other newcomers were very good, and as he sipped his beer, he thought it could go either way. He chatted with Jules and Jean about the competition as the band finished their set. The dance floor cleared, and the house lights came up. Again, Jean walked into the spotlight. As Jean was about to speak, Buck rushed by Billy with his meal ticket in tow and again, deliberately and more closely this time, brushed Billy's shoulder and glared at him as he passed by. Billy shook it off but thought the guy was going to be trouble.

After Jean thanked everyone again for coming and promised them three more great performances, she welcomed all three finalists back to the stage and greeted each one with a hug while the crowd went wild.

After the three took additional bows, Jean lined them up, and they drew straws to determine the order in which they would sing. The draw determined that Greg was up first, Billy next, and then Melanie. Billy was a little disappointed because he had really hoped for the last spot, but he was thankful he wasn't up first.

Billy and Melanie left the stage while Greg chatted with the band and Jean prepared to introduce his second song. Jean tapped the mic with her finger and said, "Singing Garth Brooks's 'If Tomorrow Never Comes,' let's hear it for Mr. Greg Ryan."

Greg started singing, and Billy knew it was going to be tough to beat him. Billy studied the crowd as Greg sang and quickly noticed that he wasn't connecting with the crowd as well as he had with his first song, which could go in Billy's favor. When Greg was done, the crowd sprang to their feet for a standing ovation that lasted at least thirty seconds.

Billy was up next, and his heart was pounding so hard he thought it would beat right out of his chest. He took a few deep breaths and attempted to calm down. He told himself this song was no different than any other song he had ever sung. It most definitely was, but he needed to ground himself before he walked out on that stage.

Jean thanked Greg for a great performance and began to introduce Billy. Billy again willed himself to relax. *Get out there and grab a hold of that audience*, he told himself. *Do what you do best. Perform.*

The last thing he remembered was Jean saying, "Put your hands together again for Louisiana-grown Billy Eagan."

The next thing he knew, he was seated in a soft spotlight with a microphone in his hand and the band playing his intro. He looked at the audience, and as the band reached the verse, he started to sing. The more he relaxed, the more he became one with the song. When he hit the chorus, the crowd went completely wild.

This must be what a drug addict feels like when he shoots up, Billy thought. *Or the high an alcoholic gets when he takes a drink.* The energy he was receiving from the audience was much like a drug or a drink, and he wanted it, he needed it, he bathed in it.

In a flash the song was over, and Jean was back onstage. The crowd stayed on their feet for over three minutes; even Jean couldn't calm them down. She was finally able to get the crowd to settle as she introduced the last performer.

Billy knew firsthand how hard it was to follow an act that affected a crowd so strongly. He had done it many times and didn't

21

envy Melanie, not because he was so good, but because the crowd would not accept anything less than perfection. Jean had told him earlier that Melanie had chosen "Take Me as I Am" by Faith Hill, so he knew she had to nail it to have a shot at winning. Jean again took the stage and said, "Ladies and gentlemen, please welcome to the boards our last performer, Melanie Dodge."

As Melanie took the stage, she was noticeably shaken. When the band finished her intro and she began to sing, her voice cracked and broke. Melanie stopped and asked the band to start again. She made it through the song, but just barely. The crowd reacted in kind, and she left the stage in tears. Billy felt terrible for her, but at the same time, he was relieved to have a little less competition.

The time had come for the winner to be announced. Jean called Billy, Greg, and Melanie to the stage, and they all shook hands, hugged, wished each other luck, and stood at Jean's left. As Jean called out Greg's name he stepped forward. The crowd erupted into a thunderous round of applause. When the audience settled back down, Jean called Melanie's name. As expected she received limited, but respectful, applause. When she finally called Billy's name and he stepped forward, he thought the roof was going to rise right off the place. Men and women alike were on their feet, waving hats and screaming Billy's name: "*Bil-ly! Bil-ly! Bil-ly!*"

In that moment everyone knew who the winner was. Greg and Melanie congratulated Billy one last time before they exited the stage. Jean gave Billy the biggest hug and said with watery eyes, "I knew you could do it, honey. Congratulations."

All Billy could do was smile and bow. When he left the stage, Jules was there with a bear hug and more congratulations. He and Jean walked Billy over to the bar with their arms over his shoulders like proud parents. Billy was overtaken with emotion and a single tear slid down his cheek, not because he had won, but because he knew his parents would be so proud of him. And he knew they would be happy he had these wonderful new people in his life too.

For Billy, the rest of the evening was heaven. He had a few more beers and relived the entire performance over and over again in his head until he finally allowed himself to accept that he was really on the way to living his dream.

Only one thing cast a shadow over the evening. He mentioned to Jean and Jules what had happened with Buck and Tina, and they were not at all surprised.

"She's at every open mic, and she never wins," Jean said. "Most nights she just looks embarrassed, but nonetheless, she's always here." She turned to Jules. "I don't like that Buck Stevens one bit. I wish you would fire him from the ranch."

"That wouldn't make him stop pushing Tina to sing here every month," Jules replied.

"Well, maybe he would leave town in search of a new job and leave that poor girl alone," Jean said.

Jules looked at Billy. "You keep your eyes and ears open and let me know if anything out of the ordinary happens. Will you do that?" he asked.

"Yes, sir," Billy agreed. Then he put Buck out of his mind and concentrated on enjoying his victory.

COMING BACK to earth—and to work—on Tuesday wasn't easy, but Billy appreciated more and more how fortunate he had been to end up with a boss like Jules. For the next few afternoons, Jules was there to help with the horses when Billy got back from the trail rides so Billy could meet with the band at Jean's.

He and the band put together a song list for the next month and spent some time rehearsing several evenings a week before the bar opened. Billy knew he had to work extremely hard if he was going to turn the opportunity he had won into a shot at a career. A month wasn't a long time. He hoped like hell it was enough time to prepare to be discovered.

Chapter Four

IAN DILLON had just finished dinner at Millie's Pub, which had become a favorite of his, and was making some notes in preparation for a recording session later that night to complete a demo for a new artist he'd recently discovered, when his cell phone rang. He looked at the caller ID and smiled. *Jean!*

"Hey. What's up, doll?"

"Hi, Ian. When you get a chance, it would probably be worth it for you to stop in and check out this new kid who won the open mic contest this week. He's been killing them ever since."

"Yeah?" Ian said. "Tell me about him."

Jean continued, "His name is Billy Eagan, and he's something else. The kid's got it all—looks, charisma, and most of all, talent. The response from the ladies has been overwhelming, and the guys even seem to like him."

"The guys too?" Ian asked jokingly.

"Oh, honey, you know guys. They especially like anyone who can get their ladies turned on," Jean said with the hint of a chuckle.

Ian laughed. "Yeah, I imagine you're right."

"Oh, and Ian?"

"Yeah?"

"I think you two would really hit it off."

Ian sighed. "Okay. I'm leaving Millie's and I've got about an hour or so to kill, so I'll see you in a few."

"Perfect."

BILLY WAS settling in to his new gig very well. This was his third night opening for Capitol Nashville recording artists Jed Strong and the Renegades, and although Jed hadn't said anything, Billy could tell that he wasn't very happy with the response Billy was getting from the crowds. He imagined it was getting harder to follow his act, but there was nothing he could do about it but be sensitive and try not to rub it in.

He stepped up to the bar to get a bottle of water to take onstage with him and noticed Jean at the other end of the bar on the telephone. He waved at her, and she returned the gesture while continuing her conversation. The house band was just starting their warm-up set, so he had about forty-five minutes before he took the stage.

Water in hand, he was heading backstage to wait for showtime when he saw a couple of the guys from the ranch walk in. He switched directions and made his way through the crowd, though not without being stopped a time or two to shake hands and smile as if he were running for office. He didn't quite understand people's sudden interest in him, but he thought it would probably fade by the end of his month-long gig.

When he reached the guys, they all exchanged greetings, ordered beers, and shot the bull for thirty minutes or so. By then it was almost showtime, so Billy said his farewells. He turned away from the bar to go backstage to freshen up, and as he did, he noticed Jean hugging a gorgeous blond-haired man who had just walked in the door. He felt a strange twinge of jealousy. Was it because it was Jean who got to hug the hottie or because she seemed so fond of him, whoever he was? Billy kept walking but made a mental note to ask her about the man later.

IAN MUST have arrived just minutes before Jean saw him. She was about to make a beeline in his direction, but he stopped to talk to someone he knew, so she waited.

As she watched him carrying on his conversation, her memories floated back to the first time they'd met, some eight years ago.

Ian had walked into the bar looking very lonely and broken. He'd just arrived in town and knew no one, so Jean had reached out to him. They'd talked for several hours while she'd tended bar, and after much conversation, she'd realized that he was a nice young man who'd had some really bad breaks, and she'd taken a liking to him. A bartender had quit that very day, leaving Jean in desperate need of help. Ian was in desperate need of a job, so it had worked out perfectly. She'd offered him the job and the studio apartment over the bar as lodgings, which he'd gratefully accepted.

The very next day Ian had moved in and started working. It hadn't taken him long, Jean remembered, to get comfortable with the rhythm of the bar business. He'd begun bartending in the late afternoons when the saloon was just opening, which helped him get familiar with the layout and learn to mix the drinks and run the register. He'd also done some bouncing on Friday and Saturday nights, but he'd told her that the part of the job he liked most was working with the performers, getting them set up and ready for rehearsals and doing sound and lighting checks.

Jean had quickly noticed that Ian had a knack for sensing who would be a hit and who wouldn't, and it wasn't long before she'd involved him in the previewing, hiring, and scheduling of new talent. Jean's impulse to help had benefited them both, and with each day she'd seen a little of the weight he'd been carrying melt away.

At every opportunity, Jean had taken special care to introduce Ian to her friends, regulars, and business contacts. And in no time at all, Ian had made quite a name for himself as her right-hand man. One night, she'd introduced him to Josh Randal, a talent scout for Capitol Records, Nashville, and the two men had hit it off right away.

Jean mostly listened as Ian and Josh talked for over an hour about all the solo artists and groups Ian had auditioned over the last couple of months. In painstaking detail he'd described to Josh who he thought was going to be a hit and who wasn't and, in his opinion, why. Later, in private, Josh had told Jean that he'd just been promoted and Capitol was looking for a replacement scout.

After many long conversations with Ian and several meetings with the label, Josh had formally offered Ian the job. He'd accepted the position with a great deal of excitement, and Jean was so happy for him, but at the same time, she'd had a heavy heart at the realization that he would no longer be working for her. She'd known that she and Ian would always be friends, but things would never be the same as they were when he'd lived there at the saloon and they worked together most every night.

They'd become very close, more than just friends, and she was, in a way, his surrogate mother. She'd been thrilled when Ian had asked if he could continue living in the studio until he found another place to live, as this living arrangement would guarantee that they would see each other just as often.

Jean was snapped out of her thoughts as Ian walked up and greeted her with a big hug and a kiss. "Sure is good to see you, honey," Jean said. "How've you been?"

Ian shrugged. "Pretty good, doll. No complaints. You look younger every time I see you."

"Oh, Ian. You're only saying that because it's true," Jean replied with a smile.

"It is true," Ian said.

Jean shook her head. "Oh, stop flattering me. You don't need a job, do you?"

"Not today," he replied. "But one never knows."

"Are you making time for any fun?" Jean asked.

Of course, she knew the answer was no, but she kept encouraging Ian to put himself out there.

"No, ma'am," Ian responded. "No time. Too much work and not enough hours in the day."

"Now, Ian," Jean said as she walked him over to her private table and gestured over her shoulder to the bartender to get him whatever he wanted to drink, on the house. "I've got a call on hold in the office, but when I get off the phone, we're going to talk about this some more."

IAN SMILED weakly and nodded because he knew she wasn't going to let this go until she'd had her say. "Yes, ma'am," he replied.

He took a seat, ordered a beer, and then sat back and waited for the show to start. Jean's table was on the back wall on the highest level and was the perfect spot from which to watch the audience and the stage.

As Ian sat there waiting for the newcomer to start his set, he thought, as he always did when he visited Jean, how much things had changed since he'd first wandered into Jean's Magnolia Saloon all those years ago.

He'd just turned twenty-one then, and he was running as far away from home—South Carolina—as he could get. He remembered watching Greenville disappear in his rearview mirror through teary eyes as he made his way out of town. So many emotions were overwhelming him: anger, love, resentment, but mostly betrayal. Those were the emotions he knew he would forever associate with being in love. He'd silently vowed never to expose himself to the possibility of such pain again. He'd looked for the shortest route out of town, and when he'd seen the entrance ramp to Interstate 26, he'd taken it and headed north. He needed to be as far away from his repulsive parents and the memories of South Carolina as his truck could carry him. But mostly he needed the distance from Todd Slocum, the love of his life, the man who had broken him so badly he would never feel whole again. He'd had no idea how he was going to deal with the blinding pain he'd felt at the hand of the man who had vowed to care for and love him forever.

He'd driven most of the night. Thirsty and in need of a bathroom break, he'd searched for an exit. As he was approaching the next off-ramp, he'd seen a sign that read Interstate 40 West, Knoxville, Two Miles. Shortly after he merged onto I-40, he saw a billboard inviting him to Visit the Grand Ole Opry, and he knew he was going to Nashville.

The first time he had seen Jean's Magnolia Saloon, it had been through eyes blurred with tears as he sat in his truck amid the neon lights of Broadway and fought overwhelming emotions. Drawn to the sign, he'd found his way to the parking lot and entered the saloon, where he'd immediately been hit by the scents of alcohol, sawdust, smoke, and the sound of Tim McGraw singing "Live Like You Were Dying." And soon after that... Jean.

JEAN LAID a hand on his arm and whispered his name.

Startled, Ian said, "Oh, Jean?"

"You seemed to be a million miles away, honey. Are you okay?"

"I was just thinking about the first time I walked through these doors. You and Jules were my first real friends in Nashville, and I owe you so much. You gave me a roof over my head and a job—not just a job, but in the end, a career that I love. A great many wonderful things have happened to me since that first night, and every time I walk through your front doors, I'm reminded of how lucky I am to have you both in my life. It seemed at the time that I had lost everything, but in reality, I found even more."

"You are a good, honest man, Ian. You're a hard worker and a hell of a son," Jean said. "Don't you ever forget that."

Although Jean and Jules had always treated him like a son, they had never really referred to him that way before. Ian suddenly filled up with emotion. He took Jean by the hand and squeezed it tightly. "I love you."

Jean squeezed back. "I love you too, Ian. Now, enough trips down memory lane. I've got a man you're gonna make famous."

Ian laughed. "So tell me about this kid's first three nights."

Jean's eyes lit up. "This type of talent doesn't come along very often, in my humble opinion. I haven't seen the entire package in a long time, honey."

"I've never known your opinion to ever be humble," Ian said with a chuckle.

"It's so different now," Jean replied. "The music business is not about the talent anymore, it's mostly about the marketability."

"You know," Ian said, "the labels want to make money and make it fast. With all the studio capabilities these days, you can make a pig sound like Patsy Cline."

Jean sighed. "I know, but I feel terrible for the young stars who sound great in the studio but sound terrible in a live concert. Just for kickers, when was the last time you heard an entertainer sound great at the CMAs? It just breaks my heart," she said. "But I digress. Back to Billy."

"I know what you mean," Ian said, "but I'm here to change that. So when do I get to see this guy?"

Jean looked up and the clock over the bar. They had been so into their conversation, they hadn't noticed the place had filled to capacity and the crowd seemed electrified. The dance floor was packed, and it was standing room only.

She stood. "No better time than now. Let's get this show on the road."

Ian watched as Jean stuck her head behind the stage, apparently to make sure Billy and the band were ready to go.

At a nod from Jean, the house lights dimmed and the spotlight hit her. "Welcome to Jean's Magnolia Saloon. Tonight we have a very special night for you. In addition to Jed Strong and the Renegades—" The crowd went wild, and Jean waited for them to quiet before she continued. "—we have a newcomer among us. For those of you who weren't here for open mic night this week, you'll be blown away by this Cajun boy right out of New Orleans. Ladies and gentlemen, please welcome Mr. Billy Eagan."

Ian wasn't sure what he expected, but his heart skipped a beat when he saw Billy take the stage.

Billy was tall, inches taller than Ian's own five-foot-ten-inch frame. His close-cut coal-black hair, accented by the stage lights, shone like velvet.

Ian took note of the long black eyelashes that shaded his deep-set crystal-blue eyes. Below his baby blues was a nose that looked like it was perfectly designed for his masculine face. His lips were full, his jaw was firm and slightly squared, and he was sporting just a hint of a five o'clock shadow. He was carrying a black felt Stetson hat with a rhinestone band and wearing a black leather jacket hanging open to reveal a shiny silk shirt tucked into place behind a tasteful sterling silver belt buckle big enough to bring attention to his slim yet muscular frame. Black Wranglers and beautifully polished black Justin ropers completed the outfit.

When Billy slipped the Stetson onto his head, Ian could feel the man's charisma as clearly as he could see his strikingly handsome face beneath the hat. His sharp features and tall muscular frame worked perfectly onstage and, as Ian allowed himself to imagine for a minute, offstage as well. *It's been so long since I've felt even a flutter of an attraction to someone. Why now?* Was he just looking at Billy as a potential new artist for Capitol, or was it something else?

Ian hadn't been a saint, of course.

In his early years in Nashville, when the pain of Todd had receded a little, and at Jean's encouragement, he'd tried to get back out there. He'd had a one-night stand or two but never even as much as a quick or casual relationship, and nothing at all in the last few years. Fear of the slightest connection to anyone left him cold and closed off emotionally. He'd adjusted to the fact that his head would never allow it. Or was it his heart? He no longer knew, and he'd given up trying to figure it out a long time ago.

Billy opened with "Find Out Who Your Friends Are" by Tracy Lawrence. As Ian watched Billy, and the crowd's reaction, he instantly noticed that in addition to Billy's physical appearance, he had that star quality very seldom seen in today's entertainers. He was able to connect with the audience with an ease that Ian seldom felt from the stage.

In a word, Ian was stunned. Billy's voice was strong and easy, his transition from upper to lower registers was as smooth as velvet, and Ian could hear just a hint of R&B in his rich tone. He sang effortlessly, and the lyrics flowed like a slow, lazy river.

Billy ended his set with the entire house, including Ian, on its feet. The crowd was screaming for more. Ian watched Billy glance off to the wings, and he saw Jed nod, so he figured Billy was looking for permission to do an encore.

31

As Ian watched, Billy walked up to the band, said a few words, and then picked up his guitar and headed back to the mic. "Ladies and gentlemen. Thank you so much for the warm reception. I would really love to end my set with the first song I ever wrote. It's called 'The Love of a Man.' It was inspired by my mother, who always said she wouldn't have had a life without my father's love."

Billy took the stool at center stage, and the spotlight found him as he hit the first note.

The song was a ballad, and Ian watched as the dance floor quickly filled with couples doing a very slow two-step. Before long the dancing stopped, and the crowd stood there quietly watching, couples holding their dance partners and rocking back and forth with looks of approval and understanding.

Ian was amazed. Billy hit note after note perfectly and sang the song with an ease that he'd rarely seen. When the song was over, the crowd applauded and yelled their appreciation. He had really struck a chord with the ladies, and there wasn't a dry eye in the house.

Ian thought about his own parents, and a tear slid down his face as well, but for much different reasons. He cleared his head and again focused on Billy. He'd seen crowds react similarly to various singers, but never at Jean's and never for a guy who had just arrived on the scene. The room was electric, but besides that, Ian suspected he would never forget that night for far more reasons than he was willing to admit, even to himself.

Billy's set was over. "Folks, I've taken up more than enough of your precious time. Let's bring out the guy you really came here to see. Please put your hands together for Capitol Records recording artists Jed Strong and the Renegades."

Ian watched Billy head offstage and meet Jed midway. The two men embraced, and Billy continued until he was out of sight. Jed thanked him for getting the crowd going and began his set.

WHEN BILLY reached the wings he couldn't believe what had just happened. He felt like he was floating on air. After four nights, they

32

still liked him! Jean was heading his way, and he sure hoped she was equally happy with his performance. In reality, he had no reasons for concern; she was thrilled and told him so. She also said she had someone she wanted him to meet.

"Now, Billy," she said, "I didn't want to make you nervous, but I invited a very good friend of mine who just happens to be a talent scout for a Nashville record label, and he wants to meet you."

"What? No way!" he said. Billy couldn't believe his ears. "Jean, are you serious? Where is he?"

Jean gestured to the corner. "He's sitting over at my table, and he's waiting for you. Take a minute, calm down, and don't be too anxious. He's a great guy, and I think you two will hit it off perfectly. I'll be over shortly."

Billy went to the men's room, freshened up a bit, took a deep breath, and headed into the crowd. He was stopped at least ten times by well-wishers with words of encouragement. But when he finally made it to Jean's table, he instantly recognized the guy Jean had been hugging at the door earlier.

The man stood. "You're a pretty popular guy right about now."

"Oh, man, I can't believe it," Billy replied with a smile.

Ian stuck out his hand. "I'm Ian Dillon."

Billy returned the handshake. "Billy Eagan. So nice to meet you," he said, pumping Ian's hand. When the pumping stopped, they looked into each other's eyes, and all at once Billy saw nothing else. The place was empty except for the man in front of him.

Billy couldn't let go of Ian's hand, and Ian didn't seem to want to let go of his either. For a brief moment, Billy felt like time stood still. He couldn't believe the warmth he felt simply shaking this man's hand. Something he had never experienced with a simple handshake before. Suddenly Billy was aware of Jean speaking.

"I see you two boys have met. Can I get you something to drink?"

"No, ma'am, thanks," Ian said. "I've already had two beers and I'm driving, so I'll pass."

"Nothing for me either, Jean," Billy added. "I'm still high from the crowd."

"Then I'll let you two boys chat, and I'll see you in a little while."

"I'll walk you back to the bar, Jean." Billy looked at Ian. "Will you please excuse me for a minute?" he asked as he took Jean's hand.

Before they left, Billy watched Ian kiss Jean's cheek and tell her he'd see her in a bit.

As Billy walked Jean back to the bar, he was grinning from ear to ear. "What's with this guy? I shook his hand, and all of a sudden, I'm seeing stars."

"Honey, he's the one seeing a star, and you're it!" Jean replied.

"Is he really a talent scout? How did you meet him? What label is he with? Does he like boys?"

Jean laughed and said, "Yes. Long story. Capitol Nashville, and yes, he likes boys. Does that answer your questions?"

Billy simply smiled.

"Now you better get back over there and charm him before someone else moves in for the kill."

"Got it! I'm on my way," Billy said as he headed back to the table.

IAN WATCHED Billy walk away with Jean and couldn't believe what had just happened. The guy seemed to be as genuine as he was good-looking and talented, and that was a hard combination to find. He took another glance in Billy's direction. He couldn't remember the last time he'd had this type of reaction to anyone and was stunned by his admission. *Stop it*, he told himself. *This is a business meeting.* Jean hadn't really told him anything about Billy except how talented he was.

Could he be gay? Surely not, but then he remembered Jean saying that she thought the two of them would hit it off nicely. *What did she mean by that?* Ian told himself it didn't matter. He was long past the point of ever thinking he could be happy in a relationship. His time for that had passed, and he was content being alone.

Just as Ian was contemplating how he should handle the situation, Billy walked back and took a seat. "Sorry about that. I've only known Jean for a short while, but I feel so damn protective of her. I hate to see her walk across the bar unescorted."

"Chivalry is not dead," Ian said with a chuckle.

"Not while I'm still alive, anyway."

Ian smiled warmly. "Jean is very lucky to have someone like you looking out for her."

"Are you kidding? She and Jules are the only real friends I have in Nashville. I'd do anything for them."

"I'm really happy to hear that, Billy. Think you can add one more to your short list of friends?"

"I can probably squeeze in just one more," Billy said through a grin. "Who do you have in mind?"

"How about me?" Ian asked.

"Done," Billy said. "Jean has spoken very highly of you, and any friend of theirs is a friend of mine."

He and Ian chatted it up, casually getting acquainted. After a while, Jean came by to make sure her boys were getting along okay, and they turned their full attention to her.

"Now what have I done in this world to have two such handsome men swooning over me?" she asked.

"Just lucky I guess!" Ian and Billy said simultaneously, looking at each other and then at Jean. They all had a hearty laugh before Jean returned to her duties.

Ian told Billy about his responsibilities at Capitol Records and how he and Jean had met some eight years ago. Of course, he didn't go into any real detail, but he hit the highlights, and in return Billy shared his responsibilities at the ranch.

Billy talked about his family back in New Orleans a bit. But when it came time for Ian to do the same, Billy noticed that he quickly brought the subject back to him. *There's a story there!*

"So?" Ian asked. "Jean tells me that for the next month, you'll be opening for Jed. How do you feel about that?"

35

"Excited and scared at the same time, if that's possible," Billy replied honestly.

"Of course it is," Ian assured him. "But you'll get used to it. You're a natural."

"Thanks."

"If you don't mind, I'll try to get a few of my colleagues out to take a look at your show, and we'll see where that leads us."

Billy about slipped out of his chair. "You kidding me? Of course it's all right."

"No promises," Ian said. "But I'll do the best I can."

"I don't know how I can ever thank you," Billy responded.

"We'll come up with something."

BILLY AND Ian continued to talk about the ranch, the music business, and everything in between until Jean came over one last time. "It's closing time, boys."

Both of them looked at their watches in amazement. Neither could believe it was so late.

"Where did the time go?" Ian asked, shaking his head.

"Not sure, man, but it sure flew by."

Both men stood up and offered to help Jean close the bar. And as usual, she refused. She positioned herself between them and walked them to the door with a hand on each of their arms.

"I'll walk Ian to his car and be right back," Billy said.

"Okay, honey, I'll see you in a minute."

Billy walked Ian to his SUV and thanked him for taking the time to stop and catch his show.

"Now this is some ride," Billy said as he admired Ian's pearly white Cadillac Escalade.

"This old thing?" Ian smiled.

"It's a thousand times nicer than my old pickup."

Ian glanced at his watch and looked startled. "Damn, I was due at a recording session five hours ago, and I totally forgot about it."

Billy felt terrible. "Oh man, I am so sorry. This is all my fault."

"Don't be ridiculous," Ian protested. "You have nothing to be sorry about. You didn't hold me hostage."

"Yeah, but—"

"Look. I enjoyed every minute of your show and our time together. If I hadn't, I wouldn't have forgotten about the session."

"Will you get in trouble?" Billy asked.

"Na," Ian said. "I'm sure they tried to reach me, but it was so loud in there, I couldn't have heard my phone ring. I'll check my voice mail on the way home. Either way, it won't be a problem when I tell them I've found their next big star."

"I sure like the sound of that," Billy replied.

"Me too," Ian chuckled. "So where were we?"

"Well, let's see, you were telling me how much you enjoyed the show and were about to ask for my telephone number."

"Now was I?" Ian asked, sounding amused.

"Yep, I remember distinctly."

"You know, you're right; I remember now. Besides, I may need to get in touch with you to set up a Capitol meeting or something."

"Just a Capitol meeting?" Billy asked, disappointed.

"Or something," Ian said while he was reaching into his truck to grab a notepad from his attaché case.

Ian handed the notepad to Billy, and Billy wrote down his number. In return, Ian gave Billy a business card. "In case you need me for anything."

Billy smiled and stuck out his hand. Ian accepted it and they held each other's gaze for what seemed like eternity. Ian seemed no more ready to let go than Billy.

Reluctantly, Billy pulled away. "Drive safely, and hopefully I'll see you again very soon."

Chapter Five

BILLY WATCHED Ian drive away and headed back inside to get the scoop from Jean and Jules. He wanted to see if they'd had anything to do with the events of the evening.

When he walked in the front door, the place was empty and the band was gone. The bartenders were busy restocking, and he heard Kitty Wells on the jukebox singing "I Can't Help Wondering." He saw movement out of the corner of his eye and turned toward the dance floor. Jean and Jules were wrapped around each other, dancing to the last song of the night.

He turned around so as to not interrupt the tender moment, but Jean saw him, motioned him over to the bar, and pointed to a stool. When the song was over, Jules and Jean walked over and sat next to Billy.

"It's been quite a night," Jules said.

Unable to control himself, Billy blurted out, "Okay, you two, spill the beans."

"What beans?" Jean asked with a guilty look.

"You know what beans," Billy insisted. "Ian Dillon? Capitol Records? How much did you guys have to do with what took place tonight?"

"Well," Jean said, "I simply called a friend of mine and asked him to stop by and see a new performer, who's also a friend. For God's sake, that is what he does for a living."

"But why didn't you tell me?"

"I didn't want to make you nervous, and I wasn't even sure tonight was gonna be the night. It all just worked out."

"All I can say is thank you," Billy said giving them both hugs. "So now that we have that out of the way, tell me about Ian."

"What do you want to know?" Jules asked.

"Everything."

Jean looked at Jules and said, "Let me see…."

Jean told Billy about the night Ian had come into the saloon and how she'd given him a job as a bartender and bouncer. And then how he'd shown an interest in and had a knack for knowing which performers had real potential. And then how he had worked his way up to selecting and hiring new talent, and finally, how she'd introduced him to Josh Randal, which ultimately got him the job at Capitol.

"Do you guys ever stop doing good deeds?" Billy asked.

"Oh, Billy," Jean said. "We just put one and one together, and we usually get two."

Jules finally got a word in edgewise. "So what else do you want to know?"

"For starters," Billy asked, "does he have a boyfriend?"

"Oh my," Jean said. "You know I don't tell tales out of church, but just between us, no."

Billy couldn't help smiling. "It's a good thing because if he did, I just might turn into a home wrecker."

Jules shook his head and they all laughed.

"You've done so much for me. What can I do for you?" Billy asked.

"For starters," Jules said, "you can get things started at the ranch tomorrow. I'm taking my little lady home and we're sleeping in."

"It'd be my pleasure," Billy said, meaning it. "But if I'm going to open up shop, I'd better get going. I have a full day tomorrow myself." They exchanged hugs, and Billy headed for the door.

When Billy reached his truck, he noticed a folded piece of paper on the windshield tucked under the wiper blade. He retrieved it, hopped into the cab, and unfolded the paper. "My business card only has my work number on it, so here's my cell and home, if you need me for anything." It was simply signed with a big *I*. *He came back to leave a note.* The thought pleased Billy to no end.

Folding the note and putting it in his wallet, Billy pulled out of the parking lot.

IN THE shadows, a man lurked unseen, an expression of profound disgust on his face.

BILLY SMILED all the way home as he relived the entire night. It was almost four in the morning and he knew he wouldn't get any sleep, but he couldn't wait to get to his bunk so he could lie there and relive the entire night in slow motion. When he reached the bunkhouse, all was quiet. The first shift usually woke about six o'clock. It was a little early, but he thought he would start the coffee for the guys anyway and then lie down for an hour or so. He took a quick shower before he crawled into his bunk and then stared at the window for any signs of dawn.

Eventually, the sun crept up over the horizon, and Billy watched the daylight finally seep into the bunkhouse. He pretended to be asleep when the first-shift crew started moving around, as he wasn't quite ready to talk to anyone. He spent the time thinking about the possibilities in both his professional and his personal life and wasn't ready to let go of the fantasy just yet.

When the other men finally left, Billy jumped up, pulled on his clothes, and followed them. By the time he reached the stables, the hands were already preparing the horses for the day's rides. After making sure all the horses were ready, he took the golf cart over to the mess hall to pick up the box lunches for the tours.

When he returned, the guides took the box lunches and placed them in the saddlebags and then took a break while they waited for the riders to arrive.

The day flew by, and before Billy knew it, all the horses had returned and been unsaddled and put out to pasture. While they enjoyed a well-deserved break and a grassy snack, Billy helped put the tack away and then hopped up on the fence to watch the horses. Glancing at his watch and noticing it was four o'clock, he reached for his wallet and took out the note from Ian, dialing the first number.

After two rings Billy heard, "Ian Dillon."

IAN'S DAY had passed in a blur. When he'd pulled into his garage the night before, his heart had still been as light as a feather, and he'd realized that since he'd left the saloon, he had been humming Billy's song, "The Love of a Man."

After a quick shower, he'd lain in bed, telling himself that Billy had just taken him by surprise and he would get this under control, all the while wondering if Billy was home yet and tucked into bed thinking about him.

His day had started at a breakfast meeting with his boss to tell him about Billy. It lasted until almost noon. He had just enough time for a quick bite before heading to the rescheduled recording session he'd missed the night before. By four o'clock he was in his SUV heading home when his cell phone rang. He looked at his caller ID, saw the 504 area code, and smiled. He opened the phone and said, "Ian Dillon."

"Ian, it's Billy Eagan."

"Hey, Billy. How are you?"

"Fine, thanks. How was your night?"

"What was left of it by the time I got home was okay. I didn't get much sleep, but what I got was great. How about you?"

"No sleep for me," Billy said. "By the time I got back to the ranch, I was afraid to go to sleep. I figured I might not wake up on time, so I just stayed up. Hey, I know this is probably a long shot, but do you have plans for tomorrow?"

"I don't think so," Ian said. "I'm driving, but hang on a minute while I pull over and check my schedule."

Ian crossed over two lanes of traffic and pulled to a stop in the emergency lane. He brought up his schedule on his phone and took a look.

"You still there?" he asked when he put the phone to his ear.

"I'm here," Billy replied.

"Oh, good. All I have is a breakfast meeting that should be done by nine thirty or so. What do you have in mind?"

"I have the next couple of days off, and I was hoping to see you."

Caution, Ian thought. *Don't do it.* "I think that can be arranged," Ian said before he could stop himself. *Damn it! Why did I say that?*

"Do you ride?" Billy asked.

"Now, Mr. Eagan. Just because I scout for country music's best talent doesn't mean I'm a cowboy."

"It doesn't matter," Billy reassured him. "I don't care what we do."

"I was just kidding," Ian said. "I do okay in a saddle."

"One of the ranch hands said there are some really great trails up at Bells Bend on the Cumberland River. You feel up for a day ride?"

"Sure," Ian said. "What can I bring?"

"Just you. I'll pack a couple of lunches, and we'll be all set."

"Sounds great," Ian said. "Where do you want to meet?"

"Can you meet me at the Lazy H, say around ten o'clock?"

"Sure."

"Perfect." Billy said. "I'll see you then."

"I'll look forward to it," Ian replied while his brain was telling him, *No! No! No!*

Chapter Six

BILLY'S REGULAR schedule gave him Mondays and Tuesdays off, but he always rose early out of habit. He started the coffee, as he often did, and inhaled the rich smell with the anticipation of his first cup. When the coffeemaker beeped, he poured his coffee, pulled the blanket off his bed, and went out to the front porch. The air was crisp and cool, and wrapped up tightly in his blanket, he sipped his coffee with the excitement of endless possibilities for the day.

He loved fall. As the sun came up over the horizon, he thanked the heavens for what he thought was going to be a beautiful day. The turning leaves were well on their way to showing off brilliant shades of gold, red, and orange. As he took in the beautiful scenery, he thought this was the perfect day for the first date he'd had in over two years. He could hardly wait for ten o'clock.

After several cups of coffee, he decided to shower and dress so he could get to the stables in plenty of time to prepare the horses. As Billy stood with the hot water running over his body, he thought about what he should wear. He wanted to look his best but not like he'd put forth any effort.

After drying off and wrapping the towel around his waist, he headed for his locker. He settled on a pair of black 501s, a royal blue shirt, his black boots, and his old black Stetson. As he was about to close his locker door, he caught a glimpse of himself and paused. *It'll have to do.*

He headed down to the stables and chose two of his favorite horses for the day's adventure. For Ian, he chose a chestnut mare

43

named Firefly; she had just the right amount of spunk but was very even tempered as well. Since he didn't know how experienced Ian was on horseback, that seemed best. For himself, he chose a beautiful buckskin Arabian named Duke, a horse he had adopted for his own shortly after he'd arrived at the ranch.

Once the saddles and tack were loaded into the horse trailer, he took the golf cart up to the mess hall, a trip he could do in his sleep, and fixed two special box lunches. He began with a little cheese and crackers for starters, turkey and cheddar sandwiches with chips as the main course, chocolate chip cookies for dessert, and a couple bottles of water. As he was leaving, he grabbed two apples for the horses. On the way back to the stables, he swung by the bunkhouse and picked up a bottle of red wine he'd been saving for a special occasion. He couldn't imagine an occasion more special than today.

IT WAS eight fifteen, and Ian discreetly looked down at his watch. He was so ready for this meeting to be over. Mentally, he had checked out thirty minutes earlier, when his presentation was complete and he had gathered all the information he needed. As the clock inched its way to nine thirty, Ian grew more impatient. Finally the meeting concluded and because today he couldn't afford to be stopped by anyone, he made a mad dash for the door. Once he reached the parking lot, he knew he was home free.

He got in his SUV, put on his seatbelt, and slid the key into the ignition. As he turned the key, he imagined the car not starting, or even worse, a dead battery. But right on cue, the engine turned over and started to purr. He sighed, put the SUV in drive, and headed to the ranch.

He couldn't believe how excited and nervous he was, all at the same time. He made a quick stop at the liquor store to pick up a six-pack of beer, and within twenty minutes, he was approaching the entrance to the Lazy H Ranch.

He'd passed under this arch many times with Jean and Jules, but it felt different this time somehow. Almost like the first time.

The thought hit him hard. He knew it had everything to do with Billy Eagan.

BILLY HAD finished all the preparations and was just about to load the horses into the trailer when he saw Ian driving down the dirt road toward the stables. His heart immediately fluttered and butterflies began to dance in his stomach. He calmed himself, rested against the stable wall, crossed his arms over his chest, and waited for the SUV to approach.

When the vehicle came to a stop, Billy stood up straight, took a deep breath, and walked over to meet Ian, who got out of his SUV with the brightest smile Billy had ever seen. As Billy walked his way, he thought how great Ian looked. He was dressed in worn blue jeans, a western-cut white shirt with the first two snaps open, which showed off just enough of what Billy knew was a well-defined chest, and brown lace-up ropers. Just as Ian was about to close the door, he reached in and pulled out a brown suede Stetson. When Ian tipped his hat in Billy's direction, Billy thought he would melt right then and there.

Ian closed the car door, and Billy was there with his hand stuck out.

"Hey, Ian, it's good to see you."

"Hello, Mr. Eagan. You look great."

Billy smiled. "You can call me Billy." They both laughed and shook hands with a tight grip.

"We're almost ready. I just need to load the horses into the trailer and we can be on our way."

"Sounds good to me," Ian said as they walked toward the horses. "Which one of these great creatures is mine?"

"That would be Firefly, the chestnut. She's a really sweet girl, and I told her all about you."

Billy was untying Firefly and heading to the trailer when he heard Ian say, "Hey, stud."

He spun around and was just about to say "hey" when he saw Ian patting Duke on the neck. He smiled and turned around quickly in hopes that Ian hadn't seen him.

"Who's this guy?" Ian asked, referring to Billy's horse.

"That would be Duke. He's my favorite, and besides he's a little sweet on Firefly, so I thought we would double date."

"Date? Is this a date?"

Billy felt his heart stop and was about to apologize when he saw the grin on Ian's face. Being quick on his feet, he switched gears quickly. "Oh, it's a date all right."

"Good, 'cause I was sort of hoping it was," Ian said.

"Now that we have that settled," Billy said. "Let's get these horses loaded and be on our way."

THEIR ROUTE to Bells Bend was incredibly beautiful. It took them up Interstate 40 toward the ridges of the Western Highland Rim and Ashland City. Once they hit the Bells Bend Park Trailhead, they had been on the road for about an hour. During the drive, there was never a lull in conversation. They discussed politics, recent events, and the music business, but as they approached the foothills, all topics took a backseat to the scenery and the breathtaking colors of fall.

After they parked, Billy unloaded the horses and began to saddle and bridle Duke. Ian followed suit with a familiar ease and did the same with Firefly. It was very clear to Billy that Ian had spent some time around horses, and he immediately felt more relaxed.

They finished preparing the horses almost simultaneously, and Billy reached into the truck and grabbed the two saddlebags he'd packed the lunches in earlier that morning. He secured one on the back of each horse and Ian shoved three beers in each saddlebag as his contribution. They were about ready to go.

While Billy secured his truck and horse trailer, Ian mounted Firefly. When Billy turned and headed toward Duke, he had to stop a second to admire the beautiful man on horseback. With the morning sun on Ian's back and the fall colors all around him, Billy thought this was a picture he would remember for many years to come. He sensed the strength and ease with which Ian mounted Firefly and realized that his earlier admission of "I do okay in a saddle" was a major understatement. They rode side by side, talking about the scenery, Nashville, the horses, and country music. As the morning passed, they became more comfortable, and the topics transitioned effortlessly from one to another, but it seemed that they both felt too vulnerable to get any more personal.

The trail narrowed as it approached the first crossing of the Cumberland River. At the ford, the river was only about two feet deep, and both horses seemed adjusted to the terrain, so Billy took the lead and they crossed without incident. Once over the river, they followed the narrow trail as it climbed to the ridge and widened again as they looked out over the hills of Davidson County. They rode a bit farther, admiring the vistas, and came across an overlook with a pavilion surrounded by a split-rail fence. Attached to the roofline of the pavilion was a gutter system that spilled into a half barrel, supplying ample water for the many horses using the trail.

"Looks like a great place to stop for lunch," Billy said. "What do you think?"

"Sure," Ian said. "I could use a bite."

They dismounted and walked over to the split-rail fence, where they tied up the horses so they could drink and cool down after the uphill climb. Once the horses had their fill of water and looked pretty content, Billy removed his saddlebag and pulled out the two apples he'd packed earlier that morning. He dug in his pocket for his pocketknife and cut one of the apples in half, handing both halves to Ian. "Firefly's been waiting for this."

He did the same with the other apple and fed each half to Duke, watching as Ian followed his lead. With the horses taken care of, it was their turn. Billy removed a blanket he had rolled and tied to the back of his saddle and turned to Ian. "Follow me." Saddlebag in hand, instead of heading for the pavilion, Billy led

Ian to a small clearing slightly off the path that he had spotted when they'd ridden up.

IAN NOTICED that the cozy clearing Billy had chosen had a slightly different view that overlooked the majesty of the Great Smoky Mountains as well as the foothills to the east. He studied Billy, amazed at the fluidity with which he moved as he spread out the blanket and began to set up a picnic lunch. The man had thought of everything. Ian could see how hard Billy was working to make this day a special one, but little did he know, Ian thought, that just being here with Billy was special enough.

Ian continued to watch as Billy moved with purpose. He was a man who seemed to know exactly what he wanted in life and was very confident that he was going to get it.

"Hey, stud," Ian said with a smile.

Unlike before, Billy didn't turn. So Ian repeated, "Hey, stud," and Billy turned slowly and smiled.

"I thought you were talking to Duke," he said.

"Yeah, well, I *was* talking to Duke this morning when you turned around, but this time I was really talking to you."

Billy's face went blood red. He smiled, swallowed hard, and said, "I don't know what you're talking about."

"Oh yes, you do," Ian teased.

"Okay. So you saw me. I'd really hoped that you hadn't."

"Oh yeah. I saw you, and it took everything I had not to laugh out loud. But I thought it would probably come in handy later in the day, so I kept it to myself." Ian walked up to Billy and gently kissed his cheek. "I thought it was very cute," Ian said. "Let's eat."

Billy and Ian finished setting up the picnic lunch and rested on the blanket side by side. Propped up on one elbow, facing Billy and the amazing view, Ian popped the top on a beer and offered one to Billy. He accepted and in return said, "I also brought along a bottle of wine, if you're interested."

"Let's save the wine for later," Ian replied.

WITH LUNCH spread out between them, Ian and Billy sipped their beer and enjoyed their meal. It was Monday, and Billy hadn't seen any other trucks or horse trailers parked in the lot, so he felt reasonably certain they were up here alone. After they finished eating, Billy packed what was left of lunch and put it in his saddlebag. With the food between them now gone, Billy slid closer to Ian and impulsively kissed him on the lips, pulled back, smiled, and kissed him again.

Just then Billy heard a noise like twigs breaking under a shoe or boot.

"What was that?" he asked as he turned his head in the direction of the sound.

"What was what?" Ian asked. "I didn't hear anything."

They were both quiet for thirty seconds or so, but they heard nothing.

Billy finally broke the silence. "It was probably just the horses."

He turned to Ian and said, "Now, where were we?"

This time Ian was the one who leaned in for a sweet, gentle kiss. With his free hand, he reached up and removed Billy's hat. Ian ran his fingers through Billy's hair and rested them at the base of Billy's neck. He pulled Billy closer, dropped his elbow, and rolled over on his back, pulling Billy down with him.

Billy broke the kiss for just enough time to stare into Ian's eyes with warmth and a need he hadn't experienced in a very long time. Holding Ian's gaze, Billy went in for a deeper, longer kiss, closing his eyes as his tongue parted Ian's lips. Ian's warm, welcoming mouth accepted Billy, and they began teasing and tormenting each other while they lay stretched out on a blanket in the late October sunshine.

When they came up for air, Ian said, "You sure do know how to kiss a man, cowboy."

"Much obliged, sir," Billy replied.

They both laughed. Billy gave Ian another peck on the lips and then glanced at his watch. "Wow, it's three o'clock already."

"Are you serious?" Ian asked.

"Yep. You need to know I could stay like this forever, man. In fact, I wish I'd packed a pup tent and supplies for a stay over, but since my stupidity prevailed, we probably need to start thinking about heading back. It'll take us a couple of hours to get down to the parking lot and another hour or so with rush-hour traffic to drive back to the ranch. That will get us back between six and six thirty."

Ian made a sour face. "All right. All right. Let's go." He gave Billy another kiss and shot to his feet. "Come on, time's a-wasting, cowboy."

THEY MADE good time on their way down the mountain. When the trail again narrowed just before the river, Billy took the lead and crossed first. When he reached the other side, he looked back to make sure Ian was right behind him.

Ian and Firefly were midway through, and Billy couldn't help but enjoy the scenery. Ian was beaming. He sat tall in the saddle, seemingly relaxed and very comfortable.

Billy smiled back at him and was about to move on when Firefly suddenly reared unexpectedly. Billy looked on in horror as an unprepared Ian slid out of the saddle and headed for the river. Billy was a little relieved when he saw Ian right himself to land on his feet.

In a flash Billy was off Duke's back and splashing through the water to get to Ian. Firefly ran to the other side of the river, where Duke was waiting, stopped, and looked back as if to say "Oops, my bad."

Ian was laughing when Billy reached him, pointing at Firefly and the astonished expression on her face. Billy was not quite ready to laugh. He had to know if Ian was all right. "Are you okay?"

"Yeah, I think so. A little stunned, but I think I'm okay," Ian answered. He tried to take a step, and his face twisted with pain. "Shit," he said, favoring his right leg. "I think I messed up my ankle."

"Okay," Billy said. "Let's keep your weight off of it." With one sweeping motion, Billy had Ian in his arms and was carrying him across the river. When they reached the other side, Billy lifted Ian even higher to help him scramble onto a waiting Firefly's back. "Can you ride?"

"I think so," Ian replied.

"Put your left foot in the stirrup and hold on to the saddle horn. I'll get you home."

A LITTLE stunned at what had just happened, Ian couldn't speak. He simply stared at Billy, trusting that he was going to do exactly what he said he would do.

Ian looked on as Billy mounted Duke, walked over to Firefly, and took the reins from him. Billy led Ian and Firefly back in the direction of the parking lot, both men soaked to the bone.

NEITHER OF them noticed the figure of a man hiding in the brush, watching the events unfold.

WHEN IAN and Billy reached the parking lot, the sun was starting to sink behind the mountain, and Billy thought the air was significantly cooler.

"Don't move," Billy said to Ian as he dismounted Duke. "I'll get the truck started and the heat going. Once I get you settled, I'll get the horses unsaddled and loaded."

"No way," Ian replied attempting to slip out of the saddle. "We'll do this together. After all, I'm the reason we're wet."

"No!" Billy insisted. "We don't even know how bad your ankle is hurt. You should keep your weight off it."

"I can manage," Ian said. "Let me at least help."

Billy saw something in Ian's eyes he couldn't quite put a finger on, but he acquiesced. "Okay, but promise me you'll take it easy. No weight on that foot."

"Deal," Ian said with a look of relief.

With Billy's help, Ian slid off of Firefly and balanced on one foot while Billy unsaddled both horses. By leaning some of his weight on Firefly and keeping his injured foot off of the ground, Ian was able to brush her down to aid in the cooling-off process. When the horses were ready to be transported, Billy secured their blankets over their backs and loaded them into the trailer.

With the horses and trailer secure, Billy helped Ian into the truck, closed the door, and ran around and climbed in the driver's side. The cab was warm and welcoming.

As Billy pulled out of the parking lot, he opened his cell phone and pressed the speed dial button for Jules. When Jules answered, Billy explained what had happened and asked him to have someone meet them at Nashville General to pick up the horses and get them back to the ranch.

"No," Ian protested as he listened to Billy's plan. "I'm not going to the hospital."

"Jules," Billy sighed. "Let me call you right back. It appears I have a stubborn patient here." Billy disconnected the call and glanced back and forth between Ian and the road. "We really need to get that ankle checked out."

"I'm sure it's just a sprain," Ian said. "A little ice and it'll be fine."

"I would feel much better if we had it looked at," Billy insisted.

"It's really not that bad," Ian said. "I appreciate your concern, but I'll be fine. I promise."

"Okay," Billy agreed reluctantly. "But since you're in such a promising mood, promise me tomorrow you'll go to your regular doctor and have it looked at."

"I promise," Ian said.

Billy called Jules back and told him not to worry about meeting them at the hospital; they would be back at the ranch in about an hour. Jules assured Billy that a couple of ranch hands would meet them there and take care of the horses so he could get Ian home.

Just over an hour later, they reached the ranch, and Sam and Buster, two of Billy's hands, were waiting for them.

"Everything okay?" Buster asked.

"I think so," Billy said. "Firefly got spooked, and Ian landed in the water."

"I'm fine," Ian yelled from the cab of the truck.

"I guess he's fine," Billy chuckled. "It would be a big help if you could take care of the horses so I can get him home."

"We got this boss," Sam said. "Do what you have to do."

"Thanks, man. I really appreciate it."

While the guys attended to the horses, Billy helped Ian out of the truck and over to his Escalade. He put him in the back with his legs stretched across the seat. Billy slid in behind the wheel, started the SUV, and began searching for the heat by pressing every button on the computerized dashboard. Seats started moving, the windshield wipers whirled, and the stereo blared Tim McGraw.

"I assume you're looking for the heat?" Ian yelled through "Indian Outlaw."

Billy smiled weakly but kept pressing buttons. He did manage to turn off the stereo as he mumbled under his breath, "I've got one blue button for air conditioning and one red button for heat in my truck. This looks like the dashboard of the frickin' starship Enterprise."

Ian chuckled and leaned forward between the seats. "Okay, press the…." Ian got Billy back to the main menu until he found the climate control screen and eventually the heat.

"Thank God," Billy hissed. "Will you be all right for a few minutes?"

"I'll be fine. Why?" Ian asked.

"Don't move," Billy said, closing the back door. "I'll be right back."

Billy quickly took the golf cart to the bunkhouse and grabbed a change of dry clothes, a pair of sneakers, and a bag of ice. When he got back he took the blanket they'd used for lunch from the horse trailer, along with his saddlebag. He opened the front driver-side

53

door and tossed the saddlebag to the passenger-side floorboard. "Still okay?" he asked over the seat.

"Still okay," Ian responded.

Billy opened the back passenger door and gently lifted Ian's right leg, placing the rolled up blanket under his ankle to elevate it. He unlaced the top few rows of Ian's boot, pulled as tight as he could on the strings, and retied the knot, hoping to keep the swelling to a minimum. He laid the bag of ice over the boot. "I don't want to take your boot off until we get you home, but the ice should help until we get there."

Billy once again slid in behind the wheel. "Let's get you home."

Ian smiled. "Whatever you say, cowboy."

Billy drove down the dirt road toward the ranch gates. It was a pretty bumpy ride, but he did his best to avoid any potholes and unnecessary bouncing.

"How's my patient doing?"

"Good," Ian replied. "But I can feel the swelling pressing against my boot."

"Are you sure you won't let me take you to the hospital?"

"Positive," Ian replied. "But do you know where you're going?"

"Come to think of it, no, I don't," Billy said. "Where do you live?"

"In Westhaven, about an hour south of Nashville. Take I-40 east to I-65 south, and I'll direct you from there."

They drove in silence for a few minutes. "Billy?" Ian said.

"Yeah?" Billy replied.

"I'm sorry about all this. Some first date, huh?"

"What are you sorry about?" Billy asked. "I'm feeling very gallant. Almost like a knight, and I think I like it."

"A soaking wet down to your boots kind of knight," Ian teased. "And you're acting like such a gentleman."

"I'm not acting like anything," Billy said. "I *am* a gentleman. And a gentleman always makes sure his date gets home safely."

"Your mamma taught you well."

"Yeah," Billy said. "But I've always been a caretaker. Ever since I was a little tyke."

"A little dyke?" Ian asked teasingly.

Billy laughed out loud. "Tyke. Not dyke."

"I know," Ian said. "I'm just pulling your leg. But in all honesty, I'm enjoying being taken care of. Is that crazy?"

"No way, pilgrim," Billy said in his best John Wayne voice.

ONCE THEY exited I-65, Ian gave Billy directions to his home. Billy turned into the driveway and stopped.

Ian lived in a beautiful three-story Colonial row house at the end of a cul-de-sac.

"The left button over the rearview mirror," Ian said.

Billy pressed the button and the garage door slowly started to open. When it was all the way up, Billy pulled in and put the SUV in park and turned off the ignition.

He helped Ian slide out of the backseat, but because the garage was under the row house on the lower level, he again scooped Ian into his arms and carried him up the flight of stairs to the main floor of the house. While still in Billy's arms, Ian opened the door, and they pushed their way inside.

Billy's eyes widened as he entered Ian's house. The door leading up from the garage opened directly into a great room the size of Billy's bunkhouse at the ranch. To the right was the living area, with a large stone fireplace on the far wall. Built-in bookcases framed both sides of the fireplace, and a large flat-panel television hung above the stone mantel. The room was painted a light golden tan and furnished with a big brown leather U-shaped sectional in the center, surrounding two large leather ottomans. Everything sat on top of a big cowhide rug that made the space seem cozy and intimate.

To the left was a very spacious kitchen, with wraparound granite countertops and stainless steel industrial appliances. The breakfast bar faced the great room, fronted by four leather-upholstered barstools with copper-studded nailheads.

Billy immediately headed for the couch and gently lowered Ian onto it. As he began to straighten, a pair of hands tugging on his shirt pulled him back down. He stopped long enough to get his balance and felt lips gently pressing against his. Ian's lips were warm and soft. Billy's tongue sought entry, and Ian welcomed him. When they finally broke apart, Billy looked into Ian's eyes, smiled, and grabbed one last kiss before he quickly straightened.

"Where's your bedroom?"

"Bedroom?" Ian asked. "Now you hold on one minute, cowboy," he added. "I'm not that kinda guy."

Billy laughed. "Seriously, man? I just want to get you some dry clothes."

Ian laughed. "Oh, is that all? I was so trying to play hard to get. Up the main stairs, second door on your left."

On the way upstairs, Billy passed a half bathroom on the right, tucked away under the stairs, and what he assumed was Ian's home office. The room was handsomely decorated with a large desk, a leather chair, and two matching side chairs.

As Billy quickly scanned the room, he paid special attention to the built-in covering the wall behind Ian's desk. It housed his computer and a CD player, but what really caught his attention was the endless supply of frames containing pictures of Ian with country music's royalty. At a quick glance, there were shots of him with George Strait, Reba McIntyre, Kenny Chesney, Martina McBride, Barbara Mandrell, Loretta Lynn.... The list went on and on.

Remembering he was on a mission, Billy hurried up the stairs and quickly found the open door to Ian's bedroom. He made his way to the door he assumed was the closet and entered a room at least sixteen by sixteen feet with wall-to-wall clothes racks and an island in the center that held drawer units on all four sides. Billy felt a little like a voyeur rummaging through Ian's closet—after all, he hardly knew the man—but he focused on the task at hand. He fumbled through some drawers and found underwear, socks, a T-shirt, and gym shorts.

When Billy got back downstairs, he found Ian shirtless and about to remove his left boot. Billy stopped for just a minute to observe the scene in front of him. *Damn, he looks good.* Ian's chest was exactly how he had imagined it: smooth, hairless, and very cut. His pumped-up arms were well defined, and Billy made a mental note that he needed to go back to the gym. When Ian sensed his gaze, he stopped unlacing his boot and looked up. His right foot, still in his boot, was propped up on one of the leather ottomans.

"Let me help with that," Billy said.

Ian looked up. "That was quick."

"Your instructions were dead-on."

Billy knelt in front of Ian and quickly finished unlacing his left boot. He attempted to pull it off, but Ian's boot and sock were still very wet, so the boot didn't slip off as easily as it would have otherwise. Eventually, it gave way. Billy removed the sock and noted Ian's foot and toes were shriveled like prunes. He wrapped his hands around the icy foot and squeezed for a minute in an attempt to warm it up.

"I'll get you dry and warmed up as soon as I get the other boot off, but I'll warn you, this is probably going to hurt," Billy said with a little bit of sadness on his face.

As he started to untie Ian's boot, he thought back to his Eagle Scout days and remembered that as soon as the boot came off, the foot would begin to swell very quickly.

"Wait a second," he said. "Do you have any Ziploc bags?"

"Yep, third drawer down on the left," Ian said.

Billy ran to the kitchen, found the bags, and turned to the freezer, filling a bag with ice and sealing it before heading back to Ian. Thankful Ian had worn laced-up ropers instead of a traditional boot, he slowly untied the boot, removing the leather laces completely to open the boot as much as possible. Ian had winced only once or twice by the time Billy was finished unlacing.

"Okay. This is it," Billy said.

"Go for it," Ian replied as Billy attempted to gently pull the boot off.

Billy's heart hurt as he saw the pain on Ian's face, but Ian didn't say a word. He closed his eyes, pressed his lips together, and held on to the arm of the couch.

Ian's right boot didn't give way any more easily than the left, and when the boot finally skidded off, both men sighed.

Billy closed his eyes in relief when Ian relaxed his grip on the couch and forced a smile.

"That wasn't so bad," Ian said as a single tear slipped out of his left eye.

Billy reached up and wiped the tear away with his thumb.

"I'm really sorry, man."

"No need to be sorry," Ian said. "It was my decision not to go to the hospital, remember?"

Billy just shook his head. "One more step," he said. They looked at each other as they simultaneously said, "The sock."

With the boot now gone, Ian's ankle immediately blew up like a balloon. His sock was stretched as tight as a sausage skin, and Billy doubted he could get it off without really hurting Ian.

"Wait, I have an idea," Billy said.

"I'm waiting," Ian responded.

"Do you have any scissors?"

"Yeah, in the office. Top left drawer of the desk."

Billy ran down the hall and fumbled through Ian's desk drawer while George Jones stared at him from the bookshelf. He found the scissors and was back to Ian in seconds. He slowly began to cut the sock away, starting at the top and working his way down, pulling the sock apart as he went. As the cloth fell away from Ian's ankle, Billy could clearly see the purple bruising starting to develop. He stopped cutting when he reached Ian's toes and the wet sock fell to the ottoman.

"Genius," Ian said.

Billy smiled. "Thanks."

With the boot and sock now off, Billy could see how bad the sprain really was.

He took the bag of ice and lightly placed it on Ian's ankle. "If I remember correctly, the routine is twenty minutes on and twenty minutes off—no more, no less."

Ian winced once more but kept his foot still.

"It's a good thing you were wearing lace-up boots," Billy said, "or we would have had to cut the boot off as well."

Ian laughed. "Tomorrow, I'm buying stock in Justin Boots."

"Let's get you out of these wet clothes. Put this on," Billy said handing Ian the dry T-shirt.

"Now the pants," Billy said. "And no wisecracks."

Ian laughed and started to unbutton his jeans.

Billy motioned for him to lift up just a little and then peeled Ian's wet jeans down over his thighs to his ankles. He removed the ice pack just long enough to slide the pants over the now black, blue, and very swollen ankle. He replaced the ice pack and slid the other leg of Ian's pants over his left foot.

When Billy looked up, Ian sat in a T-shirt and underwear. His bare legs were thick, long, and muscular and were covered in soft blond hair. Staring, Billy was startled when Ian said, "Now what?"

"You know what," Billy responded. "The underwear, but I'll give you some privacy for that move. Do you think you can manage?"

"I think so," Ian replied. "But you need to get out of your wet clothes too."

"Okay," Billy said. "I'll be back in a flash."

Billy ran downstairs to Ian's SUV to gather the clothes and sneakers he'd brought from the ranch. He went to the half bath he'd seen earlier and changed out of his wet clothes as well. When he returned to the living room in bare feet, dry jeans, and a T-shirt, Ian had his underwear changed and had managed to slip on his gym shorts.

"Good job," Billy said.

"Hey, you did most of it," Ian responded.

Billy saw a small blanket on the back of the couch and threw it over Ian's legs.

"Now," he said, "let's get a fire going to warm you up."

"How about just turning up the heat?" Ian asked.

"That would work too," Billy agreed. "But a fire will be nicer."

"I know of another way I can be warmed up," Ian responded.

"All in good time," Billy said with a sly smile as he kissed Ian lightly on the forehead. "Now that I have you secure with no chance of escape, I can take my time and torture you a little at a time."

Billy found everything he needed in a wooden box near the hearth and within minutes had a blazing fire going. Twenty minutes had passed, so he removed the ice pack from Ian's ankle and placed it in the freezer until another twenty minutes passed, when it would be time to put it back on.

He watched as Ian's eyes followed him around the room with the slightest hint of a smile on his face.

Billy brushed his hands together. "Now, let's see what I can rustle up for dinner."

"I can't guarantee you'll find much in the kitchen," Ian said, "I don't cook very often."

"I'll come up with something. Let me rummage around a bit."

Billy opened and closed cupboards and drawers and found his way to the pantry. After looking around, he came out with two jars of spaghetti sauce and a box of angel hair pasta. He opened the freezer and found a loaf of bread, then located the spice drawer and retrieved a jar of garlic powder.

"How's pasta and garlic bread?" Billy asked.

"Sounds great to me," Ian responded.

"Do you have a wine opener?"

"Yeah," Ian said. "But unfortunately, I'm out of wine."

"Not true," Billy reminded him. "I grabbed the bottle of red wine I stashed for today's ride when we switched vehicles."

"You're one smart man, Billy Eagan."

"Don't I know it," Billy said with a coy smile.

After opening the wine, Billy handed Ian a glass. "Now for some mood music. Where's the stereo?"

Ian pointed to the cabinet doors at the bottom of the built-in on the left side of the fireplace. Billy turned on the radio, which was tuned to Sirius's Prime Country. He stood back to listen to what was playing and immediately identified Ty Herndon singing "Steam." He looked over at Ian to see if he approved.

"Perfect," said Ian.

Billy went back to the couch, kissed Ian on the lips, glanced at his watch to make sure it wasn't time to reapply the ice pack, and went back to the kitchen to start dinner.

"I feel like such a slug," Ian said.

"Nonsense," Billy replied. "This is actually pretty fun. Except for the ankle part."

"Fun? Maybe for you, but I'm the helpless one, remember."

Billy rubbed his hands together. "Just the way I like it."

Chapter Seven

TWENTY MINUTES later Billy was walking toward Ian with the opened bottle of wine in one hand, a plate of pasta and garlic bread in the other, and the ice pack over his arm.

When Ian was settled, Billy went back to the kitchen and made himself a plate. They ate while in continuous conversation about the day, the perfect views, and the accident. Like clockwork, Billy removed Ian's ice pack every twenty minutes and replaced it again twenty minutes later.

When they were through with dinner, Billy gathered the empty plates and loaded the dishwasher. With the kitchen clean, Billy then positioned himself behind the couch with his hands on Ian's shoulders and began to gently rub what he knew would be sore muscles in the morning.

"Do you have any hand lotion?"

"I think there's some under the sink," Ian said. "Why?"

Billy laughed. "You ask too many questions, Mr. Dillon."

After yet another trip to the kitchen, Billy returned with the lotion, repositioned Ian with his legs at the opposite end of the couch, and put a pillow behind his head. "Just lay back and relax," Billy instructed.

He follows instructions well, Billy thought as he gently lifted Ian's feet and slid in under them. He examined Ian's ankle. The swelling seemed to have eased, but the ankle still looked like a discolored honeydew melon.

Billy squeezed a small amount of lotion into his hands, then rubbed them together to warm it up. He took Ian's foot and began to massage it gently.

"That feels great," Ian said. "I didn't realize this was going to be a full-service date."

"I'm a full-service type of guy," Billy replied.

"No, seriously. You've taken such great care of me; I don't know how I'll ever repay you."

"Right off the top of my head," Billy said, "I can think of a couple of ways."

Ian yanked his foot away.

"I'm just kidding." Billy frowned. "I didn't mean—"

"No!" Ian insisted. "Oh no, it's not that. It just tickled for a second."

"I was starting to get worried there for a second," Billy said with relief.

They were still laughing when Ian's phone rang. He looked at the caller ID and saw it was Jean. He accepted the call. "Hey, doll."

"Ian, are you okay, honey?"

"Yes, ma'am," he replied. "I'm fine. Billy has taken great care of me."

"Oh, Ian! You're just so stubborn. Jules told me you wouldn't go to the hospital."

"I'm fine, Jean," Ian explained. "And just so you guys will relax, I promised Billy that I would go to the doctor tomorrow to have it checked out. I'm sure it's just a sprain. It's feeling better already."

"Is Billy still there with you?" Jean asked.

"Yes, ma'am. And… he's quite the nurse."

"Well, I feel a little better knowing you're not alone. You get some rest and call me when you get back from the doctor tomorrow, okay?"

"Yes, ma'am."

"And give my best to Billy."

"I will," Ian replied. "Good night."

63

Ian ended the call and put his phone on the ottoman. "Jean sends her best."

"They love you, Ian, and they worry about you," Billy said. "You're very lucky to have them in your life."

"They are great people," Ian agreed. "And *we* are lucky. They love you too, you know."

Billy nodded as he finished rubbing Ian's left foot. "No way am I touching that bad boy," he said, referring to Ian's injured foot.

"Smart," Ian replied. "Now it's your—"

"Nope," Billy said, slipping out from under Ian's feet. "Tonight's all about you."

Billy stoked the fire and then refilled their wine glasses before returning to the couch, sitting next to Ian, and resting his hand on Ian's leg. He propped his feet up on the leather ottoman and leaned his head against the back of the couch. "You gave me quite a scare this afternoon. Do you know what happened?"

"Not really," Ian responded. "One minute we were walking along just fine, and then she entered the river and all was still good. But then it was like someone smacked Firefly on her hindquarter, hard, and she reacted. It all happened very quickly."

Billy hesitated before he spoke. "Firefly is very gentle, and from what I've seen, she has never reacted to anything quite like that. I mean—" Billy paused. "—she goes through rivers and streams all the time on the trail rides. Sometimes even with kids on her back. I may need to rethink that one."

"It may have just been a fluke," Ian replied. "Don't make any hasty decisions."

"It's clear something spooked her, but what?" Billy asked.

"We'll probably never know," Ian responded. "But it all turned out just fine. And besides, if this hadn't happened, I wouldn't be getting all this attention."

"We'll see about the attention you'll be getting after we get you to the doctor tomorrow," Billy replied.

"Billy, you don't have to take me to the doctor tomorrow," Ian protested. "You've done so much already. I'm pretty sure I can manage."

"How?" Billy asked. "First of all, you can't put any weight on that foot, and I don't see any crutches around. Second, you can't drive with your left foot, unless you are extremely talented. Not that it would be safe anyway. And third, how are you going to get down the stairs?"

Ian's expression darkened, and Billy could no longer tell what the man was thinking.

He studied Ian for a moment, and then it hit him like a ton of bricks. *You idiot*, he said to himself.

As the flood of embarrassment crept into his face, Billy jumped to his feet and started to pace in front of the couch, his hand on his forehead. "Oh man, Ian, I'm really sorry," he said knowing he was about to start rambling. "I shouldn't be pushing myself on you. I'm—I'm just the caretaker type. That's all. I get carried away sometimes. I'm sure you have plenty of friends you can call. Hell, Jean and Jules would be here in a flash if you needed them."

Billy stopped and patted his pockets out of habit, feeling for his cell phone. Then he remembered in all the commotion, he'd left it in his truck. "Damn."

Then he spotted Ian's phone on the ottoman. "Can I borrow this?" he asked, picking up the phone. "I was in such a hurry to get you home, I left my cell phone in my truck. I'll call the ranch and see if I can get one of the guys to drive out here and get me."

"No! Wait!" Ian said as he jumped up from the couch on one foot, got tangled in the throw, and stumbled forward toward the leather ottoman. Billy watched Ian as if he were moving in slow motion. Before he had time to think, the phone was flying through the air, and he was instinctively diving for Ian. Ian tried to get his balance as the two men landed on the edge of the ottoman, propelling it forward and leaving them on the floor with Ian on top of Billy.

Ian looked into Billy's eyes and said, "Don't go, cowboy."

Billy looked up with a wary expression on his face.

"I didn't mean.... Billy... I—I'd love your help tomorrow. I just don't want to be a burden." Ian shrugged. "I've spent the last

Scotty Cade

eight years learning to fend for myself, and I don't want to *need* anyone."

Confused, Billy asked, "Why would you not want to need anyone? Did something happen to you? Did someone hurt you?"

Ian simply shook his head. "I just don't want to be dependent on anyone," he said so low it was almost a whisper.

"Just because I offered to take you to the doctor tomorrow don't mean you *need* me to. It means I want to. Have I been acting like I'd rather be anywhere else?"

Ian looked like he was thinking about how to answer the question. "Of course you haven't. You've been incredible. But… we've only known each other for a couple of days, and well, to be truthful, I've only had myself to depend on for so many years, I'm not used to having anyone take care of me."

Ian paused. "It's been easier for me that way. For a bunch of reasons."

That one sentence told Billy more about Ian than anything he'd said to him since they'd met.

"Okay," Billy said, hoping his disappointment didn't show in his voice. "I get it. Or at least I think I get it. You're used to taking care of yourself, so I'll back off. But… you have to understand that this is just the caretaker in me. It doesn't mean that I want anything from you that you can't give," he continued. "You're right, we've only known each other for a very short time, and I don't know why, but I feel this strong connection to you. If we see one another for a day, a week, or a year, I will never pressure you to give more of yourself than you can give. That's not the kind of person I am."

"Billy—" Ian said.

But Billy put his hand up to stop him. "Please let me finish."

Ian closed his mouth and nodded.

"It doesn't take a rocket scientist to figure out that, in the past, someone hurt you pretty badly. And by the look on your face right now, I would imagine that the scars run pretty deep. Just know you don't ever have to say a word to me about what happened to you. But… if and when you ever want to tell me, I will be here to listen."

Billy waited and studied the bewildered look on Ian's face. Ian opened his mouth to speak and then closed it again. He sighed and kissed Billy softly on the lips. "Deal!" he said as he slid to one side, allowing Billy to get up.

Relieved that he'd said everything he needed to say, Billy stood and reached out to help Ian to his feet. Ian braced himself on the arm of the couch, balancing on his left foot with his right leg bent at the knee. Billy found the phone in one piece and put it back on the ottoman.

He then turned all his attention to Ian and wrapped his arms around him and held him tight. Billy felt the tension leaving Ian's body and thought, *One day I hope he trusts me enough to talk to me.*

When the embrace ended, Billy eased Ian back down on the couch, picked up the throw, and covered him again.

"C'mere, cowboy," Ian said as he tugged Billy back down with him. Billy stretched out on the perpendicular leg of the sectional and rested his head in Ian's lap. As they settled into the silence, Ian began to stroke Billy's hair, and Billy lay there for the longest time staring up at the man. "Will you tell me about your childhood?"

There was a long moment of silence before Ian said, "Not much to tell. I grew up in a very conservative Christian household with three brothers and a sister. I went to Bob Jones University but never graduated, and I don't talk to my family."

"Is it because you're gay?"

"Partly," Ian said and paused. "Now your turn."

He clearly doesn't feel comfortable talking about himself, so hell, I'll bore him into talking by telling him my story.

"I grew up in a Catholic family in New Orleans with two sisters; one has a son and one a daughter. I married at nineteen and divorced at twenty-one. My entire family still lives in New Orleans, and we're all pretty close to one another, in our own way. I talk to them a couple times a week, and they're very supportive of me and my dreams."

Billy paused to take a breath, and Ian interrupted. "Back up one minute. Did I hear 'married'?"

"Yep," Billy said.

"To a woman?" Ian asked.

Billy laughed. "Right again. I was very confused about my sexuality at the time. I was young and she was pretty, and it seemed like the right thing to do. I was the last Eagan boy in the family to carry on our family name, and for some reason that was very important to my father, so that only reinforced my decision."

"Wow!" Ian said.

Billy continued. "My mother is a sweet, fun-loving, and nurturing woman. I can talk to her about anything, and we're good friends in addition to being mother and son. And my father... well, let's just say he's a man's man. A good man, but a man's man. He started breeding quarter horses when I became a teenager, and together we did the rodeo circuit for a time."

"A real rodeo man, huh?" Ian asked. "Did you have a good relationship with him growing up?"

"I think so," Billy replied. "But what I remember most about our relationship then was trying so hard to earn his respect. Looking back now, I can see that my need for his approval and respect drove me to do most of the things I did. When my D-I-V-O-R-C-E happened, I thought he would consider me a failure, but he didn't. He just said, 'Son, if you're unhappy, then do something about it.' He had a hard time dealing with it when I came out to my family, though. I knew he still loved me, but there was a distance there. The funny thing—or the sad thing, depending on how you look at it—is after all the things I did to try and gain his respect, the one thing that worked was my moving away to chase my dreams. He said he'd never had the courage to follow his dreams, and that alone made him the most proud."

"Wow, that's quite a story," Ian said.

"I guess so," Billy replied. "There's a lot more, but I'll save it for another time."

Ian looked at his watch. "It's getting pretty late. You wanna head upstairs?"

"Are you sure?" Billy asked. "I don't mind sleeping on the couch."

"Nope, let's go up," Ian replied without hesitation.

Billy lifted his head off Ian's lap and began to stand. Ian tried to do the same, but Billy put his hand on Ian's chest and nudged him back down. "Stay put for a few minutes, and I'll be right back."

Ian smiled and nodded as Billy removed the ice pack from his ankle and placed it in the kitchen sink.

"I'm going up to turn down the bed and be back down to get you in a couple minutes."

IAN WATCHED Billy climb the stairs as his mind leaped into overdrive. *Is this man real? Why, after all these years, do I feel a connection to someone again? Why now? Do I want this? I know I don't need this, but do I want it? Am I being fair to Billy dragging him into my fucked-up head?*

Ian didn't have the answers, but for some reason, right now, he didn't care. He convinced himself to take it one day at a time and see how it played out. This thing was probably going nowhere, and it would fizzle out like a dying ember soon enough. Billy was probably just being nice to him, anyway, and wasn't really looking for anything more.

That thought made Ian relax a little. After all, he wasn't a teenager any longer; he could enjoy a man's company and not make any more of it than that. Couldn't he?

WHEN BILLY reached the bedroom, he turned down the bed and then walked over to the fireplace, which was well stocked with kindling, wood, and matches, and started a fire. He looked around and spotted some candles artfully placed throughout the room and lit each one. Taking one last look around, he started downstairs. The room looked very inviting, he thought.

He came down the stairs quietly in case Ian had dozed off, but Ian was in the same spot Billy had left him, staring at the ceiling. To Billy, he seemed to be in deep thought, almost troubled.

"Ian," Billy whispered. "You ready to go upstairs?"

"Anytime you are, cowboy," Ian replied.

69

Billy turned off the stereo, made sure the fire screen was in place to catch any stray embers, and turned off all but one lamp.

When Ian stood, Billy was at his side supporting him and giving Ian someone to lean on as they made their way to the stairs.

"Nice office," Billy said, stopping in front of the open door and peering in again. "That's quite the collection of pictures," he added.

"Yeah. All good people," Ian said. "But know that none of them is more talented then you are. They just got their breaks, and if I have anything to say about it, you will too."

"Thank you," Billy whispered. "I sure hope so."

When they reached the base of the stairs, Billy bent down to pick Ian up again, and Ian started to protest.

"How else are you gonna get up the stairs?" Billy asked. "Just let me do this. Please?"

Ian looked up the stairs and then nodded. Billy scooped him up and felt Ian melt into his chest, his face buried against Billy's neck.

Ian raised his head and sniffed. "You started a fire up here as well?"

"I hope you don't mind."

"Hell no," Ian said. "I love fires. I've always thought the smell of wood burning was so comforting. Thank you for doing that!"

Ian looked around the room in amazement as Billy placed him in his bed. "How did you know this was the side I sleep on?"

"Well," Billy said, "that's where the telephone and clock are, so I just figured this must be your side."

He sat down on the bed beside Ian. "I hope you don't mind, but I took the liberty of warming things up a little. With that ice pack on and off of your foot every twenty minutes, I know you must have been chilled to the bone. I didn't want to take you out of a warm, cozy environment and put you into a cool, dark bedroom."

"I don't mind at all," Ian whispered. "You're being really sweet. I don't deserve this."

"Everyone deserves a little attention, and don't you forget it," Billy said as he brushed Ian's cheek.

Ian leaned in and Billy felt Ian's full warm lips covering his own. He found Ian's lips hungry and forceful, making him feel wanted.

Ian leaned back on the bed and pulled Billy with him. Moving gently, without breaking the kiss, Billy lay on the bed next to Ian, careful not to touch his ankle.

Billy began to explore Ian's mouth, tasting him, taking him, making him feel alive and deserving of all he was being given. Billy broke the kiss and moved his mouth to Ian's ear. "You okay?"

"I'm better than okay, I'm great. Please don't stop."

That was all Billy needed to hear. On the way down to Ian's neck, Billy stopped to run his teeth over Ian's earlobe. Ian shook as if he had caught a chill. His neck tasted soft, sweet, and delicious.

Billy covered every inch of Ian's neck with gentle kisses while he rubbed his chest and caressed his nipples through his T-shirt. He lifted Ian to a sitting position and pulled his shirt over his head to expose bronze-colored, perfectly round nipples, well-defined pectorals, and a set of six-pack abs, all waiting to be tasted. Billy was in heaven. He made another mental note about going back to the gym.

Billy felt Ian began to shiver and hugged him tightly to try to warm him.

"It's your turn, cowboy," Ian whispered. "Off with the shirt."

Billy blushed but did as he was told. He saw Ian eyeing him as he moved away enough to cross his arms, grab the hem of his T-shirt, and pull it over his head. He tossed it across the room and returned his focus to Ian.

Ian reached for Billy again and ran his lips over Billy's already erect nipples. Billy moaned and whispered, "God. That feels so good."

Ian continued rubbing Billy's chest, flicking his tongue in and out over his nipples until Billy's shivers matched Ian's. Billy tilted his head, giving Ian more access, and as Ian slowly moved up to Billy's neck, he nibbled at every inch of Billy's skin. Simultaneously, Billy felt Ian's strong fingers running through his thick black hair.

Billy sensed Ian was having trouble maneuvering, so he gently eased Ian onto his back and straddled his waist. Billy could feel

Ian's erection through his jeans, and the sensation instantly made him hard as a rock.

While staring into Ian's eyes, Billy lifted up on to his knees and motioned for Ian to lift his hips. He slid Ian's gym shorts down and carefully off, never forgetting about his ankle. Billy again straddled Ian and positioned his ass slightly over Ian's knees, careful not to put any weight on his legs.

In that position, Billy could see Ian's dick clearly outlined in his navy boxer briefs. The head of Ian's cock rested right above the waistband, and it appeared to be perfectly shaped, thick, and evenly proportioned. Billy imagined neatly trimmed blond pubic hair and a hefty pair of balls underneath.

As he explored Ian's body, Billy's dick became thicker, filling the confined space inside his jeans. Billy curled over and buried his face in Ian's underwear, inhaling every bit of his aroma. His scent was clean and fresh, with a strong hint of his unique maleness.

Billy couldn't stop. He ran his teeth along the length of Ian's dick through his underwear and felt Ian shiver. Billy could feel his pulse throbbing as the blood flowed through his veins at breakneck speed. He felt Ian lift up just a bit, and Billy slid Ian's underwear off and tossed them to the floor.

Finally, Ian was naked from head to toe, and Billy was frozen. All he could do was stare at the beautiful man in front of him.

Ian sat up and grabbed at the waistband of Billy's jeans. "I want you naked, cowboy."

Billy gently rolled off of Ian and stood at the side of the bed. He slowly unbuttoned the top button of his jeans as Ian watched intently. Billy released the rest of the buttons on his 501s one at a time, shimmied them down to his ankles, and stepped out of them. As he removed his socks, he felt a little exposed, but Ian seemed to be enjoying the show.

Billy blushed again when he saw Ian staring at the outline of his erect cock, tucked away in his gray Calvin Klein boxers. Ian leaned over and ran his hand down the trail of black hairs fading from his navel into the concealment of his underwear, hooked the waistband with one finger, and pulled them down.

"Now step out of your underwear," Ian whispered.

Billy did as he was told and watched as Ian raised the covers, reached for Billy's hand, and gently pulled Billy back into bed. Both of them were naked now, and their breathing hushed as Ian moved his hand over Billy's bare shoulder, running his fingers gently across his flesh, then up to his head to trace his face.

Billy moved closer and was excited to find Ian's cock still hard and pressing against his thigh. Ian closed his eyes as Billy moved his other hand down Ian's body, his fingers running along Ian's soft flesh before finding his stiff cock and starting to caress it.

Ian moaned with pleasure as Billy caressed and fondled him. Billy shifted and slid down until he was looking directly at Ian's cock. Ian whimpered when Billy took him into his mouth. The long, hot cock was mind-blowing for Billy. He loved the feel of Ian in his mouth as he slid up and down Ian's shaft, curling his lips around the taut skin. Billy wanted this to go on forever.

Ian's masculine scent again filled Billy's senses as he buried his nose into the base of Ian's cock. Billy could think of nothing except making Ian happy. This second, this minute, this hour, pleasing Ian was all that mattered. He tightened his lips around Ian and slowly slid up and down his shaft, amazed at how warm and alive he felt. Billy gave himself over as Ian's cock invaded his mouth and the back of his throat. As Billy continued to pleasure Ian, the deed giving him intense pleasure as well, Ian made it clear he'd almost reached his breaking point.

"Won't last much longer, Billy," Ian whispered. "I'm so close but not ready to end this just yet. Please make it last."

Billy backed off and looked up into the most beautiful pair of piercing green eyes he had ever seen. Ian's wavy blond hair framed his face, and his smile was both seductive and wanting. Billy had better be careful because he could get lost in those eyes and not care if he was ever found.

Ian's lips were equally irresistible, and Billy slid up to the head of the bed and took Ian's mouth, gently at first, and then with a raw need he'd rarely experienced. When the kiss ended, Ian sat up and gently urged Billy over onto his stomach. Billy felt sensual kiss after sensual kiss as Ian rewarded his neck, back, and shoulders. His lips and tongue traced Billy's spine down to the curve of his ass. Ian brought his knees up, cautiously moved his injured ankle over Billy's ass, and straddled Billy's lower back.

"Be careful, Ian," Billy whispered. "Don't hurt your ankle."

Ian reached up and placed his forefinger over Billy's lips as if to silence him. "I'm okay. Just relax and enjoy this."

Billy took Ian's finger into his warm mouth and savored its taste, and Ian closed his eyes. He withdrew the finger and began to lightly rub and massage Billy's back, bringing chill bumps to his flesh.

Ian gently rolled Billy over onto his back again and eased on top of him. Billy stared into Ian's emerald eyes, imagining his head rolling back in pleasure when he came. If Billy had his way, that would be very soon.

After kissing Billy hard on the lips, Ian pulled away and began kissing his way down Billy's chest. Ian's lips found Billy's left nipple and began to tease it with his tongue. Billy arched his back and then relaxed again, and Ian tormented his nipples with bite after bite.

Ian kissed his way down even farther to the line of hair that led to Billy's belly button and continued down to his groin. Billy's dick was rock hard, and Ian kissed the tip and began to work it with his mouth. Billy grabbed Ian's hair as Ian ran his tongue up the shaft and licked the precum from the slit.

Billy moaned and gyrated as Ian slowly ran his lips up and down the length of Billy's cock. Billy caressed the hair on Ian's head, guiding him gently along his length, which was swelling with each stroke.

Ian released Billy's cock long enough to whisper, "Are you okay?"

"Perfect," Billy responded. "You feel so good. Can't hold on much longer."

"Go for it," Ian said.

Billy paused. "I'd like us to come together, if that's okay? I want to jerk you off while I'm kissing you and looking into your eyes."

"God yes!" Ian replied. He eased up to join Billy and reached over to open the drawer of his bedside table. Retrieving a bottle of lube, he flipped open the top and squeezed a dime-sized amount into each of their hands.

"Are you sure you're okay?" Ian asked again.

Billy nodded.

They were both glistening with sweat, and the air seemed charged with electricity. Billy knew he was going to come at any moment and slowly moved his hand up and down Ian's iron-hard cock. His mouth covered Ian's with long, deep, passionate kisses, but never once did he break his gaze into Ian's eyes. In that moment, looking into Ian's eyes was like seeing everything: the sun, the stars, the universe. Beyond the universe.

Billy broke the kiss just long enough to say, "God, Ian." Then he came in great rushing waves that moved through him pulse after pulse, forcing his load into Ian's hand.

Still trying to catch his breath, Billy laid his head on Ian's shoulder and licked the sweet sweat that had accumulated there. He began to move his hand faster and faster, and when he lifted his head to look at Ian, Ian's head was tipped back, his eyes shut, and his mouth open. *Gorgeous.*

Billy leaned forward and nibbled on Ian's neck, and Ian moaned softly. Then Ian tilted his head and again covered Billy's lips.

Ian moaned into Billy's mouth, and when their tongues met again, Ian's dick pulsed for the first time in Billy grasp. It pulsed again and again as Ian released his seed, covering Billy's fingers. Billy licked his fingers one by one, tasting Ian's unique flavor with each swipe of his tongue. Ian was panting heavily when he pulled out of the kiss, and they lay there against each other for several minutes. Billy was not sure what to say—not even sure if any words were adequate to express what he was feeling—and the silence told him Ian felt the same.

The room was dark except for the flickering embers of the fire and the dance of candle flame on the ceiling. The air smelled of sex, lingering around them like a fog, and the silence between them was somehow comforting.

Billy finally spoke. "You're really something."

Ian chuckled. "You're not so bad yourself."

Scotty Cade

"How's your ankle?"

"What ankle?" Ian replied with a grin.

"Let me take a look," Billy said. He reached over to the bedside table and turned on the lamp and was shocked at the size of Ian's ankle. It had swollen to the point where it looked like Ian's skin would pop at any minute.

"Damn," Billy said. "This doesn't look good at all. Stay put." Billy leaped out of the bed, stopping for a moment to stoke the fire before he headed for the bathroom.

When Billy found the bathroom light switch and flipped it on, brightness flooded the room, and he immediately shut his eyes against the intrusion. After a second he opened them and they gradually adjusted.

He stood in the middle of the large bathroom, staring at an oblong, sunken whirlpool tub in the center of the room. Beyond the tub was yet another massive stone fireplace. On either side of the fireplace were floor to ceiling palladium windows with frosted glass panes, framed by heavy gold velvet draperies drawn back with black rope tiebacks. He quickly scanned the room. To the right was a long mahogany vanity with double sinks and a closed door that, he assumed, led to the toilet. To his left, running the width of the room, was a large, glass-enclosed, natural stone shower, with dual showerheads, one at each end, and a large rain showerhead in the center.

Billy grabbed a washcloth from the towel rack near the shower and approached one of the sinks. He soaked the cloth in hot water and wrung it out, then returned to the bedroom, where he cleaned Ian and then himself. When he was done, he tossed the washcloth back into the bathroom.

"Thank you," Ian said.

Billy smiled. "My pleasure."

Billy pulled the comforter up over Ian, and in a flash he was gone again. He bounced down the stairs and within minutes was climbing them again. This time he had a fresh ice pack in one hand and a bowl of ice in the other. He pulled down the comforter, paused to enjoy the sight of Ian's naked body, and then positioned the ice pack on Ian's ankle.

76

"If I remember correctly," Billy said, "at this stage of a sprain, we should be alternating hot and cold compresses."

Ian simply stared at Billy with a look Billy couldn't identify. He thought it was gratitude, but he wasn't sure.

Billy went into the bathroom again. He turned on the faucet in the bathtub and adjusted the temperature, and then he grabbed a large bath towel from the rack near the shower and placed it alongside the soaking tub. Noticing that the fireplace had permanent logs, which he assumed were gas logs, he looked for a way to turn them on.

At the base of the fireplace, built into the hearth, was an on-off switch. He flipped the switch, and with a satisfying whoosh, blue flames shot out from beneath the logs.

Near the bathtub faucet stood a footed silver tray holding a grouping of glass bottles and jars, an assortment of candles, and a book of matches.

Billy knelt down next to the tray to read the labels, which identified various bath salts and oils. They would make for a nice bath. He chose a bottle of bubble bath and poured an ample amount into the quickly filling tub. Immediately, a froth of bubbles appeared. He lit a couple of the candles, stood, and took a quick look at his handiwork. As he was exiting the bathroom, he paused to adjust the lights for the perfect ambience.

When he returned, Ian had propped himself up on a couple of pillows exactly where Billy had left him. He was shivering a little from the ice pack, but he seemed to be relaxed and in pretty good condition, considering. Billy pulled the comforter down, gently removed the ice pack, and helped Ian to his feet. He allowed Ian to lean on him as they moved to the bathroom.

"Billy?" Ian said as they entered the room. "I need to pee."

"Okay." Billy changed direction and walked Ian to the lavatory closet. "I'll get you to the toilet, but no weight on that foot, okay?"

"Yes, sir," Ian replied.

Billy balanced Ian on one foot while he took care of business. When Ian was through, he shifted his weight back to Billy, who helped him over to sit at the edge of the sunken tub with his legs hanging over into the welcoming hot bubble bath.

Billy got into the tub and then helped Ian step in and lower himself to a sitting position. Billy stood to get out of the tub, but Ian grabbed his hand.

"Not so fast," Ian said. "Sit."

"Nope, I don't want to chance hitting your ankle. You need to be still, and if I get in this tub with you, all bets are off," Billy replied.

"Sit," Ian said again, this time more forcefully. "Please."

The look in Ian's eyes told Billy he really had no choice. Besides, he wanted to be as close to Ian as he could. He eased back down into the water across from Ian and placed Ian's foot in his lap to secure it. Ian smiled victoriously.

As Ian relaxed in the warm water, Billy stretched his legs out on either side of him, and Ian reached down and rested his hands on the tops of Billy's feet. Ian looked content, and that warmed Billy to his core.

Ian lifted Billy's right foot by the heel and slowly began to knead his calf. Ian worked his way up and down Billy's leg, massaging intently. He continued his way down over Billy's ankle and, with his thumbs, began to rub the ball of Billy's foot. Billy closed his eyes, laid his head back, and gave himself up to the pleasant sensations.

AS IAN gently worked Billy's foot, he closed his eyes and let himself drift. His mind instantly went to the sweet, sensitive man across from him. *How can someone I just met be having such an effect on me? This is not me.*

Billy had been so attentive to his every need. He'd taken care of him all day and continued to do so into the night, with a gentle and genuine touch to which Ian was not accustomed.

Ian tried to get lost in the moment, to simply enjoy what was happening, but his brain wouldn't allow it. The same thought came rushing back to him over and over again. *Can't love and can't trust.*

He had long ago decided that he could never totally give his heart to another man, never trust anyone completely again. The risk of loving, trusting, and possibly losing was far too great. The stakes were too high, and his heart, even after so much time had passed, was still too sensitive to chance it.

Why are you thinking about this? You just met the man.

They *had* just met. But for some reason, Billy was having an extraordinary effect on him. Billy had touched him in a way that almost made him want to think about things differently. He'd long ago accepted his fate. But if he were honest with himself, for the first time since Todd, he thought he might want to feel differently. *Might* was a long way from actually doing something, though. He could wish all he wanted, but the reality was that he would probably never be able to take that leap of faith.

BILLY OPENED his eyes. He'd dozed off and didn't know how long they had been in the tub, but from the look of his fingers, it had been a while. Ian was resting his head against the back of the tub with his eyes closed, and Billy couldn't resist the urge to lightly pass his hand over the melon-sized ankle.

Ian lazily opened his eyes.

"I'm so sorry, Ian. I didn't mean to wake you," Billy said, already wishing he hadn't given into the impulse.

"You didn't," Ian assured him. "I wasn't sleeping, just enjoying the moment. And besides, it actually felt good."

Billy held up one of his hands and Ian's good foot and inspected them both. "We're pretty shriveled. We better start thinking about getting you out of here and getting that ice back on your ankle."

"You're the boss," Ian said.

"Finally," Billy said. "How long did it take you to realize that?"

"Very funny," Ian said as Billy gently moved his ankle from his lap and stood. Billy took the towel he had placed by the tub and dried his arms, back, and chest, and then helped Ian to his feet, never allowing Ian to apply any weight to his ankle.

With the same towel, Billy dried the top half of Ian's body, then stepped out of the tub. He finished drying himself as Ian sat on the side of the tub once again. Billy helped him stand and used the second towel from the rack to dry Ian's butt, crotch, legs, left foot, and finally, with great care, Ian's injured ankle and foot.

Ian stood with his arms open, and Billy figured he knew what was coming. Billy wrapped an arm around Ian's waist and almost lifted him off the ground as he helped Ian back to bed.

He gently placed Ian in his spot, propped up his head and back with the extra pillows, and covered him with the comforter. After he emptied the melted ice pack in the bathroom sink and refilled it with the extra ice he had brought up earlier, he pulled the covers back and gently applied the last ice pack of the night to the tender ankle. He pulled the covers back and kissed Ian on the lips. "This should hold you for a while. I'll be right back."

THANKFUL FOR the dimly lit room, Ian smiled at Billy at the same time as he did the best he could to hold back the tears that stung the backs of his eyes. He silently watched as Billy returned to the bathroom. Minutes later, Billy crawled into bed, slid over, and snuggled in against him.

"Hey, cowboy," Ian murmured, "what took you so long?"

"Just doing my chores," Billy whispered.

"I'm glad you're back."

"Me too."

Ian removed the extra pillows from behind his back and slid down until he and Billy were face-to-face. He gently kissed Billy. "Thank you for everything today."

"No thanks needed. I wanted to do it," Billy said. "I know this probably sounds crazy to you, since we hardly know each other, but something about you makes me want to take care of you and keep you safe."

Ian, still fighting the lump in his throat, raised his arm, and Billy scooted over. Billy laid his head on Ian's chest, and Ian wrapped his arm around Billy and pulled him in close. And that was how they slept.

Chapter Eight

IAN WOKE around nine fifteen to the rumble of thunder and the patter of rain falling on the roof. He didn't know why—no one but him had ever slept in his bed—but he instinctively reached for Billy. The bed was empty, and a brief but unmistakable panic filled him.

Then he caught the smell of fresh coffee and bacon on the air and felt relief. He smiled, exhaled the deep breath he hadn't realized he was holding, and fought the urge to overanalyze. He was just about to attempt to get out of bed when Billy tiptoed into the room with a breakfast tray and a bowl of ice.

Billy was already dressed, which told Ian that he had gone out early to buy groceries for breakfast, and right then, Ian made a mental note to stock the kitchen as soon as he could walk.

"Morning, cowboy," Ian said.

"How's my patient this morning?"

"Better now, but I can't believe you went out in this weather to get stuff for breakfast."

"There wasn't a thing downstairs, and you know breakfast is the most important meal of the day."

"So what's your specialty?" Ian asked, sniffing the air.

"On today's menu we have… let's see, where do I start?" Billy grinned. "Fresh-squeezed orange juice, fresh-brewed coffee, a mushroom cheddar omelet, crispy fried bacon, and hot buttered toast."

"Wow," replied Ian. "That sounds great, but where's yours?"

"I'll get mine shortly, but first I need to check that ankle."

Billy placed the tray on Ian's lap and this time pulled the blanket and sheet up from the foot of the bed to look at Ian's ankle. The swelling had gone down considerably, but it was still very discolored. Billy put the new ice pack in place gently, but Ian couldn't help but wince.

"As soon as we finish breakfast, I'll replace the ice pack with a hot compress and try to ease the pain a little before you get up to go to the doctor."

"Go get your breakfast, cowboy, and get back up here pronto," Ian ordered. "I'm starving."

Billy obliged and headed downstairs to retrieve his tray. When he returned, he found Ian patiently waiting.

"Please eat," Billy said as he sat down on the bed.

"Not so fast," Ian said in a comic voice. "In case you don't remember, I'm naked under these here sheets, and if you're going to eat vittles with me, you'll need to be naked as well."

"No need to remind me about what you're not wearing, but I'll do as I'm told," Billy said.

Ian watched as Billy stripped down and crawled into bed beside him. Ian reached over to the bedside table, retrieved a remote, and pressed a button. A flat-panel television rose up at the foot of the bed.

"Cool," Billy said. "What other tricks do you have in this room?"

"All in good time, my friend, all in good time."

They ate breakfast as they watched Robin Roberts interview Kenny Chesney on *Good Morning America*. Kenny was touting his new album, and Robin was obviously smitten with him because she blushed and batted her eyelashes throughout the entire interview. After they finished eating, Billy took the trays downstairs, and Ian could hear him rinsing the dishes and loading the dishwasher. When he returned, he handed the telephone to Ian.

"Time to call the doctor."

"Not yet," Ian protested.

Billy shot back, "Okay, for every minute you don't call the doctor, I'm putting a piece of clothing back on until I'm completely dressed."

With that, Ian scrolled through his phone and found his doctor's number, grinning sarcastically at Billy. Billy seemed very proud of himself and it pissed Ian off just a little bit. After a brief hold and some conversation, Ian hung up the phone. "He'll see me at eleven thirty."

"It's ten o'clock now," Billy said. "So that gives us an hour and a half. How long will it take us to get there?"

"About twenty-five minutes," Ian answered.

"Good. Just enough time to get a hot compress on that ankle before I get you into the shower and then dressed."

Billy went into the bathroom and returned with another hot compress.

"We'll need to pick up a heating pad," Billy said as he replaced the ice pack and then crawled back into bed and scooted up next to Ian.

The expression on his face turned serious, and Ian prepared himself.

"Can we talk about something?" Billy finally asked.

"Sure," Ian replied hesitantly.

"Look," Billy started, "I don't know how to say this, and I'm probably going to ramble because that's what I do when I get nervous. So I'm just going to say it. Okay?"

Ian gave him a knowing glance. *Here we go. You needn't have worried about your hang-ups, Ian. Here comes Dear John!*

"I can't describe what happened between us last night. I mean, I know how I felt then and still feel this morning, and I'm not trying to make you say anything about your feelings. But we were pretty intimate with each other, and although I know we should have talked about this last night, I was too caught up in the moment to have an intelligent conversation. I feel guilty about it, so I'm saying it now. I haven't been intimate with anyone in a little over three years. I was tested for HIV two years ago, and the test results were negative. It's important to me that you know I would have never have done anything to you or with you if there was any chance that I was anything but perfectly healthy, and I'm sorry."

Wait, what? Not a Dear John. He's still worried about me. What is it with this man? It's only ten o'clock in the morning, and I already have another lump in my throat.

"Billy, don't apologize," Ian said, feeling relieved. "I'm an adult, and I'm responsible for my own behavior. But thank you for saying it."

Billy nodded.

"I don't know what happened between us, either," Ian confessed. "And I don't know where it will go. But I'm drawn to you. Your sincerity, thoughtfulness, and kindness shine through from your heart. It's real, you're real, and I haven't seen that in such a long time. For the record, it's been closer to four years for me. I was tested too, and the results were negative as well. Also for the record, no one has ever slept in this bed besides me. And now you."

Billy seemed to be genuinely touched. The expression on his face was sincere. He leaned in and gently brushed his lips over Ian's, then settled in for a long, hot, passionate kiss.

They stayed in that position, making out like teenagers, for more than twenty minutes. Ian kept running his left hand through Billy's thick, dark hair while holding him tightly by the back of his neck with his right, not wanting to let go. Billy explored every reachable inch of Ian's body without breaking their kiss, and Ian loved it.

"If we don't get up, showered, and out of here, I'm afraid you won't be able to pry me out of this bed," Billy said when they came up for air.

"You'll get no complaints from me, cowboy. Who needs a doctor?"

Billy smiled. "If you think you're going to kiss your way out of a doctor's appointment, you're mistaken."

"Busted," Ian teased. "Okay, let's go. The sooner we get out of here, the quicker we can get back."

"Now you're talking," Billy whispered, pulling the covers down to the foot of the bed and removing the now-cool compress from Ian's ankle and then helping Ian into the bathroom.

"Billy," Ian said. "You've got to leave me alone for a minute. There's something I need to take care of, and you can't help me with this one."

Billy seemed to understand and helped Ian over to the water closet. From there Ian hopped his way inside and closed the door.

BILLY WENT over to the shower and turned on both faucets. He noticed a control panel just outside the shower door that said Steam Shower. It had an On/Off button and a timer. *This looks interesting*, he thought. He pressed the On button and set the timer for thirty minutes.

Finding where Ian stored the extra linens, he retrieved two bath towels and two washcloths. When he opened the shower door to place the two cloths on the built-in seat, the steam was already building, so he quickly closed the shower door again.

Billy was hanging the bath towels on the rack when he heard Ian emerge from the water closet. He hopped halfway across the room, where Billy met him and helped him into the shower. Ian sat on the seat with Billy towering over him as the hot water and steam consumed them both.

Billy lathered up a washcloth and tenderly washed Ian's back, neck, and shoulders, and then he put the washcloth down and knelt in front of Ian. He lathered both of his hands, raised Ian's left arm and washed his armpit. He then ran his hands down Ian's arm and soothingly massaged his left hand. When he was finished, he did the same with the right. Motioning for Ian to stand, Billy washed Ian's cock, then slid his hands around and lathered his ass. As he ran his hands between Ian's buttocks, he felt Ian tense up.

"Sorry," he said.

"It's okay," Ian replied. "It's just been a long time since anyone's had a hand there, but don't stop."

That gave Billy carte blanche to explore and please. Wasting no more time, he lifted the head of Ian's cock to his mouth and wrapped his lips around it. This time Ian didn't tense up but gasped and placed his hand on the back of Billy's head.

It was definitely a mouthful, and Billy was enjoying every inch of it. He started to take some long, deep strokes, bobbing his head back and forth as Ian's gorgeous cock came to life in his mouth. Ian moaned and tightened his grip on the back of Billy's head. He gently pushed him down again and again.

Billy decided to give Ian's cock a rest and explore his balls. He continued to massage Ian's ass while he took his balls into his mouth and teased them with his tongue. Billy slid his fingers up the crease of Ian's ass, working them into his smooth crack until he felt his opening. He slowly teased it with his index fingers and could feel Ian flexing his ass muscles in reaction to the pleasure.

Soon Billy began to test Ian by slowly pushing a finger inside and then removing it before slipping it in again, fucking him gently. Billy again took Ian's cock into his mouth; Ian moaned and began to fuck his face. Billy decided to take a chance and push his finger all the way inside in hopes of quickly finding his sweet spot. Ian began to moan even louder, and within seconds he was shooting his warm load down the back of Billy's throat.

Right on target. Billy slowly slid his finger out of Ian's ass while he continued to suck his dick until he had drained Ian of everything he had to offer.

Ian sat down, pulled Billy close to him, and covered Billy's lips with his own. He stopped just long enough to say, "Let me take care of you."

"Too late," Billy said, looking into Ian's eyes.

He glanced down, and Ian followed his lead. Without ever touching himself, Billy had shot his load on Ian's left foot.

"I'm sorry," Billy said apologetically. "That was just so damn hot I couldn't control myself. And just so you'll know, that's never happened before. I've never been so turned on that I didn't need to touch myself to come. That was a new experience for me, and I damn well liked it."

Ian smiled sweetly, with just a hint of satisfaction in his grin all through their shower. He continued to tease Billy as he helped Ian dress.

Billy carried Ian down two flights of stairs and helped him into the Escalade.

"Don't think you're going to carry me around the doctor's office," Ian warned.

"I understand," Billy said. "But please promise me you'll at least lean on me to keep the weight off that foot."

"I promise," Ian agreed as Billy pulled out of the driveway.

Chapter Nine

IAN'S ESTIMATE of twenty-five minutes was right on the money, and they arrived at the doctor's office with a few minutes to spare. An hour and forty-five minutes later, Ian was negotiating his way through the office on crutches, his ankle wrapped up tightly and Billy carrying a set of X-rays showing a bad sprain but no broken bones. Ian's doctor was certain it would heal normally, but he'd given him a set of X-rays in the event he wanted to see an orthopedic specialist for a second opinion.

Ian said he'd be working from home for a while, so Billy had insisted on stopping at a grocery store on the way home to get some real food, as he called it, as well as several bottles of wine.

While Billy was in the store, Ian called Josh, explained the details of the accident, and let him know he would be working from home for a week or so.

Next he called Jules and Jean and waited while they figured out how to put him on speakerphone.

He also gave them a full report and answered questions about medications, healing times, and if there was any chance of permanent damage.

And then Jules said good-bye, and Jean stayed on the line. In a way that only she had with him, she slid into her next question. "And Billy? Is he still taking care of you?"

"He amazing, Jean," Ian said. "I swear if I wasn't so damaged, I'd give that man a run for his—"

Jean interrupted him. "You're not damaged, Ian, you were just betrayed and hurt. Badly."

By everyone I loved.

"But I've always felt you could move past that if the right guy ever came along," Jean continued.

"If there was ever a right guy, Billy could very well be him. I mean, I haven't felt so close to someone so fast since—well, you know."

"Todd?" Jean asked.

"Yes, ma'am, but why do you always make me say it?"

"I know you hate to hear his name, but I make you say it because I want you to know how far you've come and to reassure you that he didn't destroy you. He set you back but didn't destroy you."

"Okay, okay," Ian said. "But this scares the hell out of me, and I don't know what to do about it. Right now he's in the supermarket making sure I have enough to eat. He helped me around the house and even carried me up and down the stairs. He's dressed me, fed me, taken me to the bathroom, alternated hot and cold compresses on my ankle day and night, and dammit, I'm enjoying the hell out of it."

Ian could almost hear the smile on Jean's face, but all she said was, "That's good, honey. I think he's a good man, and if he wants to take care of you, let him."

"But—"

"No buts, Ian," Jean insisted. "Don't. Mess. This. Up."

"Thanks for the vote of confidence," Ian said.

Ian heard Jean sigh over the phone. "I know you, honey," she said. "If he's gets too close, you're gonna find some reason to run."

Ian didn't respond. He had no argument. Jean was right. She was always right. But he was broken in a way that he didn't think could ever be fixed, and he just couldn't risk another betrayal. And isn't that what people you love do? They eventually betray you.

As if reading his mind, Jean broke the silence. "Ian. Not everyone hurts you. Not everyone betrays. Have Jules and I ever hurt you?"

"No," he replied, and it was the truth. They hadn't, and somehow he knew they never would, but other people weren't Jules and Jean.

"Just promise me you won't make any stupid decisions, and you'll take it one day at a time."

"I'll try" was all Ian said.

And he wasn't lying. He would try. He'd only known Billy for two days, but he sensed down somewhere deep in his heart that Billy was a good guy.

"Besides," Ian added, "it probably won't last. So why should I be stressing out about it. Right?"

"That's the spirit," Jean said. "Always the positive one."

"Here he comes," Ian said. "I've got to go."

"Remember what I said."

"I will. I love you, Jean."

"I love you too."

Ian turned in his seat as Billy opened the back of the SUV and started loading it with bags and bags of food.

Ian smiled at him. "Are you feeding an army?" he asked.

"Na. Just you."

"By the way, Jean sends her love and thanks you for taking such good care of me."

"She's such a sweet lady," Billy said.

"Yep, she's a doll."

Billy closed the hatch and climbed in behind the wheel. They looked at each other and smiled, but neither said a word as Billy pulled out of the parking lot.

They made one more stop at the CVS to pick up a prescription for pain medicine and a heating pad and then went back to Ian's.

Billy helped Ian out of the SUV, but Ian was determined to make it up the stairs on his crutches alone, without Billy's help.

"You can't be here every minute of the day and night," Ian said. "I need to be able to do things on my own."

"You're right," Billy said. "So take it slow, and I'll be right behind you in case you fall."

In case I fall? Someone's offering to catch me if I fall. That's a new one.

"Promise?" Ian choked out as he approached the landing to the stairs.

"I promise," Billy said.

Ian slowly made his way to the top of the first floor stairs with Billy on his heels. He climbed up steadily, one step at a time. When he stepped onto the top of the landing with his left foot, gained his balance, and pulled both crutches up behind him, he sighed with a sense of accomplishment. "How was that?"

"Great job," Billy said, reaching around Ian to open the door.

Ian hobbled to the couch and sat down rather shakily. He leaned his crutches beside him and took a deep breath. "These things are going to take some getting used to."

"You'll adjust in no time," Billy yelled as he disappeared through the doorway. Ian heard him bouncing down the stairs to the garage. He watched as Billy managed to get all the groceries up the stairs in three trips and had them put away in no time.

Billy walked over and placed a little white pill and a glass of water on the table in front of Ian, taking a long look around the room. He plugged the heating pad in under the couch and left it on the seat next to Ian.

To Ian, it appeared that Billy was trying to make sure he had everything he needed before he left. He turned his head away, trying not to show any concern. *I don't care if he leaves. He's gonna leave anyway.*

Billy scanned the room once more. "Oh," he said, finding the remote and placing it on the table next to the pill and glass of water. "Do you have your cell phone?"

Ian patted his pocket. "Right here."

"Well, handsome," Billy said with his hands on his hips. "This should hold you until I get back."

He said "get back." He's coming back!

91

"Sure, I'll be fine," Ian said with a sense of relief in his voice that even he could hear but hoped Billy hadn't picked up on. "Where are you going?"

"Now let me finish before you interrupt, okay?"

Ian nodded.

"Well, I was thinking. If you want me to, I could stay here for a couple more days, just until you can manage on your own, and if I do that, I'll need a few things from the ranch. My toothbrush, for one thing, and some clean underwear, to name a couple."

Ian opened his mouth to object, but Billy held up his hand.

"You promised," he said.

Ian closed his mouth, and Billy rushed on. "I know you didn't invite me. And if you'd rather I didn't stay, I totally understand. But I'd at least like to prepare your meals for the week before I go. That way all you'll need to do is warm them up in the microwave. And of course, I'll stop by every day and make sure you're okay. I would prefer to stay and take care of you, but I don't want to crowd you. It's totally your decision," Billy concluded, a little breathless.

It must have been the adrenaline, or the events of the last two days coming together in an awful storm, but tears started running down Ian's cheeks. No matter how hard he tried to stop them, he couldn't, so he just let it all go.

Billy immediately moved closer with a look of concern on his face. "Ian? Did I say something to upset you?"

Ian couldn't answer but shook his head.

Billy put his arms around Ian and held him. "It's just the adrenaline, Ian. Once, I almost cut my finger off, and I was fine until after the stitches were in, and then I bawled like a baby. Just let it go."

Ian couldn't stop the tears. He sobbed into Billy's shoulder as Billy held him tightly, finally breaking the embrace to grab a Kleenex off the table.

"You must think I'm a complete nutcase," he said. "Of course I want you to stay, but even if I told you I wanted you to go, you weren't leaving without cooking my meals and making sure I'd have everything I needed. Besides Jean and Jules, I've never met anyone sweeter than you are."

Billy lifted Ian's chin with his finger and looked intently into his eyes. "There are plenty of good people in this world who want— no, *need*—to do the right thing. I am one of them, but know I wake up every morning and look at myself in the mirror. If I don't like the man I see, I try to become a better man. Because when it comes down to it, we all have to love who we are before we can expect anyone else to love us."

Ian took Billy's hand. "Thank you."

"Anytime. We okay now?" Billy asked.

"We're good," Ian replied. "I'll be fine. Now get out of here so you can get back before rush-hour traffic."

"One more thing," Billy said. "I've got a full load of tours the rest of the week, so I'll need to take some of them myself, which won't put me back here until at least six or six thirty every evening. And starting tomorrow, for the next four nights, I'm back at Jean's opening for Jed. You think you'll be up for joining me? You can sit at Jean's table and not have to move until I finish my set."

"I'll be fine during the day, and I think I would enjoy seeing you at Jean's. Besides, I'm quite sure I'll be ready to get out of here by then."

"So you'll be bored just enough to want to watch my show, huh?" Billy asked with humor in his voice.

"Oh! That came out all wrong, didn't it?"

Billy laughed. "Sort of, but I knew what you meant. So we have a plan?"

"We do indeed," Ian replied.

"If it's okay to use your SUV, I'll see you in a couple of hours, then."

Ian heard the garage door opening, the engine of his SUV coming to life and then fading away, and the rumble of the garage door closing again. When the hum finally stopped, the house was suddenly silent.

After taking the pill, Ian propped his foot up on the ottoman, laid his head back against the couch, and closed his eyes. He couldn't ever remember his house being so quiet, even in the beginning. He remembered how hard it had been to get used to the silence after living above the saloon for so long, but eventually he'd adjusted. For some reason, now, the silence was suddenly deafening again.

He'd bought the place at the urging of his accountant, who'd convinced him that he needed a write-off, or he would have been happy to stay above the saloon for as long as Jean and Jules would have him. But in the end, they, too, had urged him to move on, convincing him it was time.

Ian opened his eyes and stared at the ceiling of the massive room. This was much more space than he needed, and sometimes he secretly yearned for the tiny little room over the saloon, back when life had been so uncomplicated. No stuff. Just a roof over his head and the people who would turn out to be the closest thing he would ever have to a real family again.

This was certainly a great house, but Ian had never really considered staying here long term. It never felt like home, but he didn't think any place would.

But for some odd reason, having Billy here for the last couple of days had made the slightest difference. Ian couldn't put his finger on it, but maybe he was finally ready to explore the possibility of not being alone for the rest of his life.

What's happening to me? This is crazy!

Ian's mind was running rampant. He'd acknowledged long ago that since losing Todd, he'd always overanalyzed things to the max. How could he not? The way his entire life had fallen apart was still as confusing to him today as it had been when it happened. With no other choice, he'd accepted it and done his best to try and move on.

So he'd thrown himself into his work and ignored everything else. He'd done very well careerwise, but his personal life was nonexistent. Until Billy Eagan charged into his life like a bull on steroids and suddenly Ian was looking at everything differently.

Two days, Ian! It's been two days!

Ian thought back to the way he'd been acting the last couple of days, and it certainly wasn't like him. He'd always been content to be alone. He took care of himself. He didn't need anyone. He'd long ago given up on a man to love him, a couple of kids, and the white picket fence. Why was he all of a sudden considering possibly allowing someone into his life? Someone who would probably hurt him again? Logically he knew he shouldn't do it, but he didn't feel in control of his emotions anymore. He was smitten with Billy, and no one was more surprised than he was.

The pain pill slowly got the best of him, and he drifted off to sleep midthought.

BILLY DROVE Ian's SUV toward the Lazy H Ranch in silence, thinking about what had happened over the past couple of days. Damn if Ian Dillon hadn't touched his heart.

Up until now, Billy had been so career-driven and concerned about keeping his sexuality quiet that he hadn't dared date or have a sexual relationship with anyone. In this business you could never really tell who anyone was or whom they knew. He'd heard stories about guys getting their big break and then being outed by some scorned lover or, worse, by a one-night stand selling a story to the press.

One particular incident popped into his mind where it was rumored that an up-and-coming male singer was arrested in a public restroom for propositioning a police officer for sex. Whether it had been true or not, it had brought down the man's career, and he'd never really recovered from it.

Billy wondered what would drive a man to such measures. He'd never been the type to have casual sex anyway, but with the exception of Jean and Jules, he'd been especially guarded about his sexuality since he got to Nashville—until yesterday, that is.

As he drove Billy thought about Ian's reaction to being cared for over the last two days. It was clear that Ian had been a loner for some time, and there had to be a reason behind that. Billy figured someone had hurt him very badly, and he had never gotten over it. But if that was the case, what did that mean for them? If Billy pursued Ian, was there a chance for them? And if there was a chance for them, how would Ian affect his career? Would it hurt his chances of getting a break?

Billy knew that eventually he would have to decide these things, but for now, he just wanted to get to know Ian. He didn't know where it was going, but he was going to enjoy the journey.

When Billy got to the ranch, he headed right to the bunkhouse to gather his things. Sam, Buster, and a few of the other guys from the early shift were already off work, enjoying a beer and discussing what they were going to fix for dinner.

Sam and Buster already knew what had happened because they were the ones who had taken care of the horses when he'd gotten Ian back from Bells Bend. They must have shared the story because everyone greeted Billy and immediately asked about Ian.

Billy explained the diagnosis and how Ian would have to stay off his foot for about a week as he walked over to his locker, opened it, and began to rummage around for what he needed. After he packed his bag, he told the guys he was going to bunk over at Ian's house to give him a hand until he was back on his feet.

As he was walking out the door, Sam offered to cover for Billy if he needed to be away, and the others offered to do anything they could if Billy needed them. He thanked them sincerely but assured them everything was under control and that he would see them around six the next morning.

While Billy was walking back to the SUV, Buster ran up beside him and walked along with him. He looked like he wanted to say something, so Billy stopped. "Is something wrong?"

"I don't know. Maybe," Buster said. "Look, I don't know if this is anything or not, but Buck was in here earlier laughing and talking about how the queers were up at Bells Bend having a quaint little lunch and one got thrown off his horse."

"Really," Billy said. "Now how would he know that?"

Buster continued, "What you do is your business, but I just wanted you to know. Watch your back, Billy. That guy has got some serious issues."

"Thanks, man. I'll keep an eye on him. I really appreciate you telling me."

Buster nodded and walked back to the bunkhouse as Billy got in the SUV and headed back to Ian's.

Chapter Ten

IAN WAS awakened by the sound of the garage door opening and realized Billy must be home. He sat up, wiped his eyes, and ran his fingers through his hair. *How bad do I look?* Ian was reaching for his crutches when Billy walked through the door with a black leather bag and a great big smile.

He dropped the bag by the staircase, walked over to Ian, and kissed him on the lips. "Hey, handsome." Billy pressed his finger to the tip of Ian's nose. "You are very cute when you first wake up. I assume you got a little rest?"

"Hey, cowboy," Ian said in a sleepy voice. "Yeah, I think so. What time is it?"

Billy looked at his watch. "Right before six. How's the foot?"

"Right now it feels pretty damn good; it must be the pain pills."

Billy sat down next to Ian and put his arm around his shoulder. He kissed Ian again and pulled him in close.

"Would it be too weird if I said I missed you while I was gone?" Billy asked.

Ian smiled. "A little. I mean it's only been two days. And… we are grownass men. But if the truth be told, I missed you too."

Billy smiled and kissed Ian again.

"Good to know. Oh, and the guys at the ranch asked about you."

"That's nice of them," Ian said, squirming a little and reaching for his crutches. "Can you help me up? I really need to pee, and I want to change my clothes. These tight jeans are killing me."

"Yeah, but they make your ass look damn hot," Billy said as he helped Ian up and made a point of looking at his ass. "If you don't mind, I'll change too, now that I have some clothes here."

"Sure," Ian replied.

Once Ian was steady on his crutches, Billy picked up his bag and closely followed him up the stairs. When they reached the bedroom, Ian went directly to the bathroom and Billy took the clothes out of his bag.

He kicked off his boots and quickly changed into a pair of flannel pajama bottoms and a sweatshirt. Ian emerged from the bathroom with his jeans unbuttoned and open and made his way over to the armoire. He opened the massive doors, retrieved a pair of sweats, and sat on the side of the bed. He looked at Billy with his best puppy-dog eyes, and Billy smiled. "Need help?" he asked.

"If you don't mind," Ian responded.

When the jeans were off and the sweats were on, Ian sighed. "Thanks," he said. "I feel so much better."

"Me too," Billy agreed. "If you're up to it, why don't we go back downstairs, and I'll light a fire and pour us a glass of wine."

"Sounds perfect," Ian said.

Before Ian could pick up his crutches, Billy had him in a bear hug. "This is nice," he whispered. "I've been so focused on my career that I'd forgotten what it's like to spend time with someone."

Ian felt the same way, but he kept it to himself.

"Come on, I'll help you downstairs," Billy offered. "Don't want you wearing yourself out too soon. You'll need your strength for later."

"My hero," Ian said as he relied on Billy for help.

When they reached the main floor, Billy led Ian to one of the stools at the breakfast bar. He took a pillow from the couch, placed it on the stool next to Ian's, and lifted his ankle, gently placing it on the pillow. Then he leaned over and kissed Ian gently.

"Don't start something you can't finish, cowboy."

"That will have to hold you for now," Billy said as he straightened up and made his way around the bar to the kitchen. He opened a bottle of wine and poured them each a glass.

"Now what?" Ian said.

"I'm going to start a fire, and you're going to keep me company while I start dinner."

"And… what are we having?" Ian asked.

"That depends," Billy responded with a wink. "Is there anything you don't like?"

Ian looked up at the ceiling while he contemplated the question.

"I hate anchovies. No fishy fish and no animal parts I can't identify. Other than that, I'm good."

"That's good, because we're having shrimp Creole over brown rice," Billy said as he fumbled with the kindling and started the fire.

"You're really good at that," Ian said, watching the fire come to life. "I'm impressed."

"Aww, shucks."

For a moment Ian allowed himself to imagine sharing his home with someone but stopped midthought and shook his head to erase the image. *Stop it, Ian. This is crazy.*

Billy was now looking through Ian's CD collection, but he apparently saw Ian shaking his head out of the corner of his eye.

"Is something wrong?" he asked.

Still bemused, Ian didn't immediately respond.

"Ian?"

"What?" Ian asked. "Oh, sorry. Did you say something?"

"Are you still with me, buddy?" Billy asked.

"Yeah. I just got lost there for a minute. I'm back now."

"Anything you want to talk about?"

"Nah," Ian said, desperately wanting to change the subject. "Did you find anything you like?"

Billy looked at him like he knew Ian was struggling with something, but instead of pushing the issue, he simply asked, "How about Michael Bublé?"

"Good choice. He's a favorite of mine!"

Billy loaded the CD, checked the fire, and joined Ian at the breakfast bar. He placed both hands on Ian's shoulders and gently kissed the back of his neck. Ian relaxed and melted into the kiss. He turned to face Billy, and they exchanged a long look. "Thanks for that," Billy said. "But time's a-wasting."

Ian smiled. "What can I do to help?"

"Just sit there and look handsome," Billy replied.

"Oh, that's easy," Ian teased. "But eventually I'll need something hard to do."

"And eventually you'll have something hard to do, if you get my drift."

"I like the way you think, cowboy, but how long is eventually?"

"As long as it takes me to prepare shrimp Creole, meat loaf and mashed potatoes, and red beans and rice with Italian sausage. That should do it for the rest of the week," he said with a smile on his face.

"Geez! All that," Ian said with a disappointed look on his face. "I'd better shut up and let you get to it, or we're gonna be here all night."

BILLY DID a mental review of everything he'd purchased at the supermarket and then poured them each a little more wine. He opened a hunk of sharp cheddar cheese and some crackers and put them on a plate to keep Ian occupied while he started to prepare the meals.

They were both quiet for a few minutes, and Billy noticed that Ian was fidgeting like he wanted to talk about something but wasn't sure if he should.

Ian sliced a piece of cheese, placed it on a cracker, and offered it to Billy. While Billy chewed, Ian took a sip of wine and swallowed. "So... uh," he asked nervously. "Have you had any lasting relationships?"

Now Billy knew what the fidgeting was about. "Well, I've only had one, and it lasted about three years."

"I'd really like to hear about it, if it isn't too hard to talk about."

"No. I don't mind at all," Billy said. "And by the way, to you my life is an open book. You can ask me anything, and I'll do my best to answer honestly."

"Thanks," Ian responded. "So...?"

Billy thought back and started the story.

"I was twenty-one, and it was shortly after my divorce. I started going to the only gay bar I knew, but I'd drive around the block over and over again and then leave because I was too scared to go in. That routine lasted a few weeks, but one night I said the hell with it. I parked around back and walked in. I was so nervous. I stayed all of two minutes. The next time, I ordered a beer, took one sip, and then left again."

Billy looked up and Ian was staring at his wine glass as he moved it in a circular motion on the surface of the bar.

Ian glanced at him. "I'm listening," he said. "Go on."

"Finally, the next time I attempted to try my luck at a gay bar, I had a couple of drinks before I left home, which calmed my nerves enough for me to find the courage to sit at the bar and stay for a while."

"And that's where you met?" Ian asked.

Billy nodded. "His name was Steve. He was a schoolteacher and cute as a button."

"A professional man," Ian said. "Very interesting."

Billy chuckled. "It all happened in a weird sort of way, but one night I was sitting at the bar when a very attractive blue-eyed blond named Larry sat down next to me and asked if he could buy me a drink. I nervously accepted and we talked for hours. Larry, who I found out later that night was also divorced, was officially the first man I ever picked up or was picked up by."

"You slept with him that night?"

"Of course not!" Billy replied. "We met at the bar a few times, and then he asked me to his house for dinner. And... I stayed over for the night. I know, I was a slut, but what can I say. We started a casual relationship, and I soon figured out he was one messed-up puppy. We saw each other occasionally because that was the only bar I felt comfortable frequenting, and one night while we were having a drink together, he introduced me to Steve."

"So Larry introduced you to Steve?"

"Yep, and we had an instant attraction. He asked me out, and after a few dates, we took our relationship to the next level, and boy was I hooked."

"You started dating?"

"Sort of," Billy said. "We saw each other a lot, but unbeknownst to me, Steve was... how do I put this? Promiscuous. He didn't really want a monogamous relationship but didn't bother to tell me that."

"Ouch!" Ian said.

"Yeah, well, it gets worse. Instead of running for the hills like I should have, I tried to change him. I mean... if I was in love with him, then he must be in love with me, right?"

Ian raised an eyebrow.

"I know. It took me a little while, but I realized that as long as I threw myself at him and waited in the wings for his attention, he'd walk all over me. Once I tired of that and finally moved on, he saw the error of his ways and was ready to date only me, or so he said. We ended up being together just about three years, and old trusting Billy was the only one in the entire gay community who didn't know he was sleeping with every man who breathed."

"That sucks," Ian said. "I'm really sorry."

"You know, I was just so in love that I didn't see any of the warning signs. Even after I found out he was sleeping around, I continued the relationship, hoping he would change. I finally grew a pair and found the courage to end it. We tried to get back together a few times, but it wasn't the same. I couldn't love a man I couldn't trust, and I'd finally had enough. It was a very difficult and painful time in my life, which nearly killed me."

"I'm so sorry you had to go through that," Ian said.

"Thanks. It was tough, but I survived. My mother believes that everything that happens to us in life makes us who we are, and I believe it too. I didn't then, but I do now. For many years after my relationship with Steve, I didn't trust anyone, and as I said, I couldn't be in a relationship with someone I didn't trust, so I just stayed single. By the time I matured enough to learn to trust others, I was used to being alone. So I just stayed that way."

"I so get that," Ian said with a certain tone that caught Billy's attention.

"Besides, by then I had made a choice to chase a career in country music and thought it best that I simply lay low. I didn't want photos of me in a black leather thong popping up at the CMA awards."

Ian chuckled. "I'd like to see that picture."

"Trust me," Billy assured him, "it doesn't exist. Are you sorry now that you know my entire nutcase story?"

"Of course not," Ian replied. "You've been through so much. How do you get beyond the things that broke you down?"

Billy thought about the question before he spoke. For some reason he thought this was an important moment, although he didn't know why. "I deal with them," he simply said. "One at a time, until I've worked through them and they make sense to me. Don't get me wrong, I'm still cautious and protective of my heart, but I've learned to read people, and I think I've become a pretty good judge of character."

BY THE time Billy's story was over, the meat loaf was in the oven, the mashed potatoes were in the fridge, the red beans were simmering on the stove, and the shrimp Creole and a piping hot loaf of bread were ready to serve.

Rather than trying to get Ian moved, the two men ate side by side at the bar. "This is incredible," Ian said after the first bite. "Who taught you to cook like this?"

"My mom," Billy admitted.

"To Mrs. Eagan," Ian said, holding up his glass.

After they finished dinner and Billy started to load the dishwasher, Ian sat quietly, seemingly deep in thought. Billy was certain he'd shared too much with a man he'd known for such a short time, but he had no regrets. Ian asked and he answered.

"So why now?" Ian asked out of the blue.

"What do you mean, why now?"

"You said because of your career aspirations, you decided not to get involved or even date. So why now?"

"Good question," Billy said. "I asked myself the same question while I was driving to the ranch."

"And…?" Ian asked.

"The only solution I came up with is you!"

"Why me?"

"I don't know. Maybe I was always open to it if the right person came along. But he never did, so it really didn't matter."

"That's an awful lot of pressure," Ian said.

"No. It's really not," Billy replied. "I know now that my feelings are just that. My feelings. No matter how much I want you to like me and to want to see where this goes, I can't force that on you. If you don't feel what I feel, there's no pressure. I love myself enough to take care of me. And… you should do the same."

Ian sighed. "I get where you're coming from, Billy. I do. But I haven't dated in years. I decided long ago that I would keep myself buried in my work and that was all I needed. After meeting you, I'm realizing I was wrong, dead wrong; work is not all I need. And I feel like I want to see where this is going, but I'm just not sure how to do that."

"Simple," Billy said. "Day by day."

"You're so open, Billy. With everything. You face your demons head-on and get them out of the way. I wish I was more like you."

"This demon-facing, as you call it, didn't happen overnight. After Steve I was an emotionally wounded, codependent man. One day I woke up and just couldn't get out of bed. I spent the entire day curled up in the fetal position with thoughts of ending it all. By day's end, I finally gave in and downed a bottle of over-the-counter sleeping pills with a glass of Scotch. Looking back now, I realize how fortunate I was that it wasn't enough to kill me; just sure as hell made me sicker than I've ever been."

"You tried to kill yourself?" Ian asked with sadness in his voice.

"I don't think I wanted to die. I simply wanted the pain to go away. When the sickness was over and my body was on the bathroom floor, exhausted from heaving, I finally gave in and came apart at the seams. I sobbed for hours and simply let it all go. When I had no more tears, I dragged myself into the shower, and with the steam surrounding me like a fog and the hot water beating down on me, I said to myself, 'No more.' And from that time, I've spent every day of my life exploring my feelings and trying to be a better man. I look at each new day as a day of self-discovery, and you can't imagine how very liberating that is. When you hit rock bottom, there's no way but up."

Ian was silent and seemed to be processing everything he'd just heard.

Billy held off as long as he could, and then he spoke. "Ian, you didn't ask for my opinion, but I'm going to give it to you anyway."

Ian again gave him a raised eyebrow but didn't stop him.

"I think you've kept your feelings buried for so long, it's probably easier to let them stay there. I remember those days well, but please trust me on this. You may think it's easier that way, but eventually, it will be the emotional death of you."

"You're right, Billy," Ian said. "I'm not there yet, but you give me hope. We all have baggage, and of course I have a history of my own. A very painful history, and having not completely dealt with it, I know I'm not ready to share."

"And I'm not asking you to," Billy said. "When you're ready, I'll be here, but I don't want you to tell me anything out of obligation. I've already figured out that someone hurt you badly. I can see it in your eyes, and I can hear it in your words, but it's up to you to want to get over it. I can't do that for you. Maybe trying to bury the hurt just isn't cutting it; maybe you should start to think about dealing with the feelings instead of burying them."

"All I really know right now is you inspire me to be a better person. I want to feel again. I want to do this. But please be patient with me."

Billy sighed and squeezed Ian's hand. "I'll be patient as long as you need me to be. As long as it's healthy for me."

"I can't ask for anything more."

Billy put all the food away and turned off the kitchen light. He turned off the CD player and put the screen in front of the fire, which had gone out sometime back. "I guess that's it."

"We're done?" Ian asked.

"I think so."

"Hallelujah!" Ian said. "Can we go upstairs now?"

"I thought you'd never ask," Billy said, helping Ian off the barstool and following him upstairs.

Chapter Eleven

BILLY WAS on Ian's heels until they reached the hallway, where he overtook him and disappeared into the bedroom. When Ian rounded the corner, Billy scooped him up into his arms and didn't flinch when the crutches hit the floor with a loud thud. Billy pressed his lips against Ian's in a crushing kiss as he carried him to the bed.

Ian felt Billy gently sit him in an upright position on the edge of the bed. And as Billy began to straighten, Ian pulled his sweatshirt over his head. Following Ian's lead, Billy did the same to his.

Billy nudged Ian to lie back and then slid Ian's sweatpants down to his ankles. Ian's sweats came off and then his sock. He looked up to see both flying over his head and Billy standing in front of him removing his own pants. And then he knelt between Ian's legs.

All Ian could think about was Billy. This man with the hot, muscular body wanted him. Ian gasped when Billy began to nibble at his already stiffening cock through his underwear, turning his head to the side and running his teeth up and down the shaft, teasing and tormenting with every stroke.

Ian began to slowly raise and lower his hips in response to Billy's actions. He felt the waistband of his underwear being pulled down and hooked under his balls. In one tantalizing move, Billy's mouth slid all the way down to the base of Ian's cock and gradually slid back up again. He started to move up and down in slow, even strokes, and Ian could no longer control the moans escaping his lips.

Ian wanted Billy's lips on his, so he tugged on his upper arms and pulled Billy up to him. Ian plunged his tongue into Billy's mouth and consumed every ounce of passion Billy was giving him. Then a sense of panic overtook him. He realized in that very moment that he wanted Billy more than he had ever wanted anyone before. But his mind was flooded with fear, guilt, and uncertainty. Could he chance hurting Billy? The man was so open, so vulnerable, so willing to risk getting damaged.

How could Billy be so unafraid of what the future held? After all, they'd only known each other for a few days. These feelings seemed illogical to Ian, but he decided he was through trying to make sense of things. He was more certain than ever that he did want Billy, but could he make it happen? Could he forget the past and love again? He didn't know, and at this very moment, he didn't care. With so much uncertainty ahead, he just wanted to get lost in this moment. Selfish or not!

BILLY KISSED his way down Ian's chest and washboard abs to what waited below. He took Ian's erect cock into his mouth and caressed it while he gently lifted his legs. Releasing Ian's length from his mouth, he ran his tongue over Ian's balls and down the crack of his ass to his opening. Billy supported Ian's legs over his shoulders, spread Ian's asscheeks, and slowly licked and teased Ian's opening. The sweet whimpers of pleasure escaping Ian's mouth drove Billy wild.

"Do you trust me?" Billy asked in a very soft voice.

"Yes," Ian whispered.

"I want to be inside you so badly."

The silence was deafening. *He's not ready!*

And based on all he knew about Ian, he thought he understood why.

"I want you," Ian said finally.

"No pressure, Ian," Billy asserted.

"I know," Ian said as he smiled up at Billy.

Billy reached for the bottle of lubricant on the bedside table and laid it on the bed. "Condoms?"

"We don't need them," Ian said. "You told me you were safe and I trust you."

Billy slowly repositioned Ian's legs, taking extra care, and placed Ian's bandaged ankle over his shoulder and propped Ian's other foot against his chest. He lubricated his fingers and slowly started to massage Ian's opening.

Billy felt Ian tense as a finger slowly penetrated him. He imagined that Ian was probably fighting off some strong memories, and he hoped he could make this a new experience just between the two of them.

Billy heard Ian take in a deep breath and felt him relax around the intrusion as he gently probed him. Billy made sure to take his time, carefully moving and massaging to get Ian reacquainted with what was coming and to make sure he was relaxed enough to accept him.

"Are you ready?" Billy asked.

"Yes!" flowed breathlessly from Ian's mouth.

Billy positioned his length against Ian and slowly pushed into him. He heard a gasp and stopped to allow Ian time to accept his girth. Billy remained still for a few minutes and then slowly started moving again, until his dick disappeared into Ian.

He watched Ian's face and recognized the moment the pain turned to pleasure. He witnessed Ian swallow hard and take deep breaths as he relaxed into the ride. When Billy saw the transition was complete, he began to move in and out, slowly at first and then increasing the pace as he went.

"You feel so good," Billy whispered, taking hold of Ian's cock, which seemed to get harder with each thrust. He felt Ian wrap his good leg around Billy's torso and grab hold of his biceps.

Billy looked down at Ian. His head was thrown back, his eyes were closed, and Billy couldn't believe how much he yearned for this man. *Too much! Too soon!* But he covered Ian's lips with his own again just the same.

As Billy repositioned himself and his cock penetrated deeper, Ian gasped into his mouth, but he kept up with the pace.

Billy spread some lube on Ian's dick and began to slide his hand up and down, over the head, down the shaft to the base, and back up again. Ian was so hard in his hand, Billy feared he might burst any minute. Billy's balls begin to tighten, and he knew he was just over the horizon. He started to pick up speed and willed his hand to match his pace stroke for stroke as he jerked Ian off.

Within seconds Billy and Ian simultaneously shot their loads, Ian over his stomach and onto his chest as far as his chin, Billy filling Ian's warm insides. Out of breath and exhausted from the intense lovemaking, Billy collapsed on top of Ian, and they lay there in silence.

They had just gone to a place neither of them had imagined, and there was no reason to believe that they could ever turn back. Billy finally broke the silence.

"Ian?"

"Yeah, cowboy?"

"I think that was the best sex I've ever had."

"You think?" Ian said.

"Let me rephrase that. I know that was the best sex I've ever had."

"That's better," Ian said.

Billy allowed himself to slip from Ian, and he repositioned himself, this time at Ian's side. He relaxed his head on Ian's chest, and Ian wrapped his arm around Billy and held him tightly. Billy gently caressed Ian's chest and teased at his nipples.

Eventually, Billy helped Ian to the bathroom and they cleaned up and climbed back into bed. They lay there spooning, with Ian's back tucked against Billy's chest and Billy surrounding him with protective arms.

Chapter Twelve

THEY WERE in the same position when the alarm clock sounded. Obviously startled, Billy sat upright.

"It's okay cowboy, just the alarm clock." Ian reached over, turned off the alarm, and pulled back the covers, attempting to get out of bed.

Billy put a hand on Ian's shoulder. "Where do you think you're going?"

"To start the coffee while you shower," Ian replied.

"Don't be silly," Billy said. "I'll get a cup at the minimart around the corner. Please stay in bed."

Ian lay back down and Billy kissed him on the cheek. "Thank you."

Billy climbed out of bed, Ian watching his naked body. *He's got the prettiest ass I've ever seen.*

After grabbing his bag, Billy made his way to the bathroom. Ian pulled the covers up around his neck and listened to the unfamiliar sound of water cascading off another person's body, a sound he hadn't heard in over eight years. He decided he liked it; the effect was warm and comforting, strange and familiar at the same time.

Ten minutes later his cowboy came out of the bathroom. Billy's towel-dried black hair was slicked back, and he was dressed in tight blue jeans and a plaid western shirt.

Billy walked over to Ian, leaned over, and gently kissed him. "I'll call when I stop for lunch, and I'll be back here no later than six thirty this evening."

Ian mumbled, "I'll be fine, cowboy. Enjoy your day."

Billy looked around and found Ian's crutches on the floor where they'd fallen the night before. He laid them alongside the bed quietly and left the room.

Ian contentedly rolled over and fell asleep almost immediately. He woke to the ringing of the telephone.

"Hello," he mumbled.

"Ian, honey. It's Jean. Did I wake you?"

"What time is it, baby cakes?" he said sleepily.

"Ten thirty," Jean said. "How's that ankle of yours?"

"Ten thirty? *Shit*! Ah, it's doing much better, thanks. Those pain pills knocked me for a loop, though; I can't remember the last time I stayed in bed past eight o'clock."

"You need to rest that ankle anyway, honey. Don't you worry about it. I just called because Jules told me Billy had to be at the ranch this morning early, so I wanted to make sure you were okay and didn't need anything."

"Thanks, Jean, I'm good. Billy made me plenty to eat and he'll be home about six thirty. If I feel up to it, I may join him at the saloon tonight for his show."

"Oh, that will be great. I can't wait to see you both."

"Jean?"

"Yes, honey?"

"Thanks."

"For what?"

"Just being you."

"Oh, I can't help that, now, can I? See you tonight."

"See you later, baby cakes."

Ian hung up the phone. *Home? Did I just tell Jean that Billy would be "home" at six thirty? Oh man, I've got it bad.*

He got up, hopped over to the bathroom, and turned on the steam shower. While he waited for the water to heat up, he unwrapped his ankle, which looked and felt much better this morning. He stepped into the shower and allowed the steam and hot water to relax his body. As he stood under the rain shower, Ian decided that, physically, he felt pretty good. His ass was a little tender—that was to be expected after such a night. But to his astonishment, emotionally, he was okay.

He had crossed a line with Billy that he hadn't intended to ever cross again, and he was still okay. In fact, he was better than okay— he was great. *Day by day, Ian!*

Ian rewrapped his ankle, dressed, and made his way downstairs on his crutches. On the breakfast bar was a note from Billy.

> *Good morning, handsome. There's fresh coffee in the pot, a breakfast sandwich in the microwave, and a container with leftover Shrimp Creole in the fridge. Or if you'd rather, feel free to help yourself to anything in there, and don't push yourself too hard today!*
> *Billy*

Ian set the microwave to a minute and a half and pressed Start. He poured himself a cup of coffee, and when the microwave dinged, he put the breakfast sandwich on a plate and hopped to the breakfast bar. As he ate, he planned his day. He couldn't drive, nor did he have a car, so he wouldn't be leaving the house. He would first check in with his assistant to review his calendar. He would make a few phone calls, return some if he had any messages, and use the downtime to listen to the stack of demo CDs he'd neglected for the last couple of weeks. And if he was scheduled to attend any important meetings, he could join in via conference call.

He crutched his way to his home office and fell into his leather chair. He looked around and realized he would manage just fine working from home for the next few days until he could drive again.

Chapter Thirteen

BILLY MADE it to the ranch in fifty-five minutes. Jules was already there and offered him a cup of coffee.

"How's our boy?" Jules said between sips.

"He's doing pretty well, considering," Billy said.

"I've never seen Firefly get spooked like that; do you know what did it?" Jules asked.

"I have no idea," Billy replied. "One minute she was fine, the next she was on her hind legs and Ian was in the river. It was the damnedest thing."

Jules said, "We might want to keep her off the trails for a couple of days to see if anything's up with her."

"I agree," Billy said. "I'll put her out to pasture for the day and start getting the other horses saddled and ready to go. It's damn near eight o'clock."

"Good idea," Jules agreed. "By the way, me and a couple of the boys are heading down to the lower forty to repair some fencing. I'll catch up with you this afternoon."

"Thanks for letting me know. Have a good day," Billy said.

The first half of Billy's tour was uneventful. He pointed out vistas and landmarks and any wildlife he spotted, but mostly he rode in silence and thought about Ian.

When they arrived at the lunch spot, Billy put out the spread and told everyone to help themselves. He dug his cell phone out of his pocket as he walked away.

"This is Ian."

"Hey, handsome."

"Hey, Billy. How's it going out there in the Wild Wild West?"

"Oh, about the norm. Pretty uneventful," Billy replied.

"A little less exciting than the last ride you were on, I would imagine."

"A lot less exciting, and I'm happy to keep it that way, especially if you're involved," Billy said.

"Now stop being a mother hen. And… and thanks for the coffee and breakfast."

"Anytime," Billy said. "No one can accuse me of not taking care of my man."

"I certainly can't," said Ian.

Wait! Was that a smile I heard in Ian's voice? Was it because I said "my man"?

"How's your day going?" Billy asked, and he focused on the sound of Ian's voice.

"Pretty good. It's amazing how much I can get done from here. I've made a few calls and sat in on a meeting via conference call, and this afternoon, I'm going to put a big dent in the backlog of demo CDs I've been neglecting."

"Don't you go and find anyone better than me on that bunch of CDs, mister," Billy said with a twinge of jealousy.

"No chance, cowboy. I'm counting on you and that voice of yours to get me a big bonus and maybe a promotion."

"Wow, no pressure there, huh?" Billy asked.

"Maybe a little," Ian chuckled.

"How's the ankle?"

"It's much better this morning. The black, blue, and purple have mostly turned to yellow, which is a sign of healing according to the Internet, and a good bit of the swelling has gone down, so I think we're on the road to recovery."

"Damn! I was hoping to take care of you for another week or so before you kicked me out."

"Look at the bright side," Ian said. "I could always have a relapse."

"I guess there's always that slim chance," Billy replied in a sad voice. "Remind me to put a banana peel on the stairs."

"Ha-ha," Ian teased. "And by the way, no one's kicking you out. I'm getting used to having you around."

"Really?" Billy shot back.

"Yep," Ian said.

"Oh, Miss Scarlett! You act on me like a tonic," Billy said in his best Frank Kennedy voice from *Gone with the Wind*.

"Oh stop it, Frank. You say the sweetest things," Ian replied, laughing.

"So you think you'll feel up to coming with me to Jean's tonight?" Billy asked.

"Yeah. I'm actually looking forward to it."

"It's a date, then," Billy said. "I better get this lunch picked up and these people safely back to the ranch so I can get home to you."

"Sounds good. Bye, Billy."

"See ya, handsome."

Billy ended the call and starting walking back to his group. *Did I just say "home" to Ian? Oh man, I've got it bad.*

THE SECOND half of Billy's day was as uneventful as the first. He whistled his way through the rest of his chores as if he were on autopilot. He carefully helped his staff unsaddle and brush each horse, replaced the bits and hackamores with halters, and led them, two at a time, to the walker for a cooldown period.

While the horses were cooling, he sorted the tack and put it away, dumped a bucket of feed into each stall, and helped fill the water buckets. When the horses were settled in for the night, he went to the bunkhouse to pick out something to wear for the night's performance. Looking back to make sure he'd closed his locker, he nearly ran right into Buck, who was coming in the door.

Buck gave him a familiar scowl and drawled, "How's your B-O-Y-friend?"

"What's it to you?" Billy asked, not totally caught off guard by Buck's comment, thanks to Buster.

"Everyone's talking about your boyfriend's freak accident. He should be a little more careful."

"That's funny. I've been here all day, and no one's mentioned a thing about it to me," Billy barked.

"All I know is that your little boy toy better be more careful when something smacks his horse in the ass," Buck hissed.

Billy thought for a second and decided to keep his mouth shut and simply walk away. He would deal with this tomorrow after talking to Jules. He was back in the Escalade a little after five and on his way to see Ian.

IAN'S DAY had gone by very fast. He'd spent a good bit of time on the phone with Josh, talking about Billy. Josh respected him and his opinion a great deal, so it didn't take much to convince him to come out to Jean's to catch the show and to bring his wife Suzie, whom Ian really liked. He thought about whether he should tell Billy before or after the show but decided he had a right to know before he performed and would tell him when he got home.

He spent the biggest part of his afternoon, as he had planned, listening to demo CDs. After listening to each one, he sorted them into three stacks. The first and smallest stack was the ones he liked and would pass along to Josh for a second opinion. The second stack was the "maybes," and these he would listen to again in a few days to see if he still thought they had a shot before he gave any of them to his boss. And the third and tallest stack was the "rejects."

Ian hated the rejects because he knew he was throwing away someone's hopes and dreams, and no one should have the ability to do that to another person. But unfortunately it was the business, and a tough business it was. Only the best of whatever the trend was at the time would make it. He had seen beautiful people without great voices make it big because of their looks and marketability. He'd also seen people with incredible voices not make it because they

118

didn't have the look or the figure or the savvy to carry it off. It always seemed so unfair to him, but the music business was anything but fair.

He wondered how well Billy knew the business he was getting himself into and vowed that if Billy would let him, he would help guide his career and make sure he was never taken advantage of.

Ian had taken the last demo CD out of the player and was inserting it into its paper sleeve when he heard the hum of the garage door opening.

"Lucy, I'm home," Billy shouted with a strong Cuban accent as he entered the house.

"I'm in here, Ricky," Ian shouted, trying to sound like Lucille Ball and failing miserably. With a garment bag in hand, Billy stood in the doorway to Ian's office.

"Hey, stud," Ian said with a smile.

"Hey back," Billy answered. "And enough of that 'stud' stuff, okay? Am I ever going to live that down?"

"Probably not. But I'll cut you some slack because I haven't seen you all day."

"Thanks a lot," Billy said as he walked around Ian's desk and got down on one knee to kiss him tenderly.

"I've been waiting for that all day," Billy said when the kiss was over.

Ian smiled. "You really did have an uneventful day if this is all you have to look forward to."

"Very funny," Billy said as he studied the three stacks of CDs on Ian's desk.

"How'd it go?" he asked, referring to the stacks.

"As well as could be expected," Ian replied.

"Let me guess," Billy said as he pointed to the stacks in order. "Good ones. Okay ones. And not-so-good ones."

"And how did you come to that conclusion?" Ian asked.

"It makes perfect sense to me that since there are only a handful of new, really good performers, they would be the smallest stack. And it's also pretty obvious that there are so many aspiring performers without the 'wow' factor that they would be the largest stack, and with those two figured out, I guessed at the middle one."

"Well done!" Ian said. "Now take a seat because I have something to tell you, and you have to promise me that you won't get mad."

Billy thought for a second. "I promise. And do you want to know why I promised?"

"Sure," replied Ian, puzzled.

"Because at this stage of our relationship, I'm too in lust to get mad. And besides, I wouldn't want to 'mad' myself right out of another night like last night, now, would I?"

"Good point," Ian said.

"So out with it," Billy ordered.

"My friends Josh and Suzie Randal are coming out to Jean's tonight to catch your show," Ian nervously uttered.

"Josh Randal?" Billy mumbled. "Why does that name sound so familiar?"

"Because he's my boss, and if he likes you, he can make stuff happen."

"Are you shittin' me?" Billy asked.

"Nope," Ian said.

"Hell, I'm not the least bit mad. I'm ecstatic," Billy replied. "Tell me more."

"Nothing more to tell," Ian said. "I can't really guarantee anything except that he'll be there and he'll be watching."

"I don't need any guarantees, Ian," Billy said. "The fact that you went to bat for me is more than I could have asked for. I can't believe this."

"Believe it. Hopefully we'll get him there, but the rest is up to you."

"*We* didn't get him there. *You* got him there, and now I've got to figure out a way to repay you."

"Oh, that! Yeah, we'll figure something out," Ian said with a cunning smile. "What time do we need to be at Jean's?"

"I go on at nine. So about eight thirty should be fine," Billy replied.

"It's six forty-five now. That gives us a little under an hour to eat and shower," Ian figured.

120

"We better get a move on, then," Billy said.

By seven forty they had eaten, showered, and dressed, and Billy was backing down the stairs one step at a time, facing Ian as Ian proudly descended the stairs without Billy's help.

Chapter Fourteen

THEY WERE walking into Jean's by 8:40 p.m. to a packed house. Billy didn't see Jean or Jules, but one of the waitresses met them at the door.

"Hey, boys," she said. "Jean's not here yet, but she said for Ian to sit at her table, and she'd join you as soon as she introduced Billy."

"Thanks," Ian and Billy said simultaneously.

They made their way to Jean's table. Billy led the way, moving barstools and excusing himself as he asked people to step aside to allow Ian on his crutches to pass.

"Thanks," Ian said as they reached Jean's table.

"No problem," Billy answered. "If you'll be all right for a minute, I'll go to the bar and get us a drink. What would you like?"

"I'll have a Bud Light longneck."

"Coming right up," Billy said.

It wasn't long before Billy was back at the table with two beers and a basket of popcorn. He handed one of the beers to Ian. "Here you are, sir," he said as he placed the basket of popcorn on the table. He then proceeded to down half of his beer in one gulp.

"Wow! I'm impressed," Ian said.

"Don't be," Billy said. "I needed something to take the edge off. I hate to admit it, but I'm a little nervous."

"That's one way to do it," Ian said with sympathy in his voice. "Don't worry! You'll be great."

The lights dimmed, and Billy saw Jean walk onstage, followed by the spotlight. She stopped in front of the microphone stand. "Good evening, all. I'd like to welcome you to Jean's Magnolia Saloon. For all you first timers, I'm Jean, and I own this joint. So if you need anything, I'm always around. We have a great lineup for you tonight, starting with our headliner, Capitol Records recording artists Jed Strong and the Renegades."

Loud applause and whistling filled the saloon. "And opening for Jed is newcomer Billy Eagan." Before Jean could say another word the place went nuts.

Billy looked at Ian and smiled. "You think that's for me?"

"It's for you, all right," Ian said.

It finally quieted down enough for Jean to say, "Well, since you're already up on your feet and making a lot of noise, stay that way and welcome to the boards... Mr. Billy Eagan!"

"Go get 'em, cowboy," Ian said, placing his hand on Billy's shoulder and squeezing a few times.

Billy made his way through the crowd to the waist-high stage. He turned around and, with his arms bent at the elbows, used the palms of his hands to boost himself up and land on his butt on the edge of the stage. He pulled the mic stand down, removed his mic from the holder, and tipped his hat as the band started the intro to his opening number.

During the first week of rehearsal, not knowing why, he'd picked a cover by Rascal Flats called "Bless the Broken Road" as his opening number. He'd never sung it before and had never been particularly drawn to it, but at that moment in time, he'd felt some connection to it, so he went with the feeling. When he started to sing the lyrics, seeing Ian in the audience, he knew why he'd chosen it.

IAN WATCHED with respect and admiration as the crowd responded to Billy, perched on the edge of the stage singing his heart out. So much so, that he felt a quick pang of jealousy at the thought of having to share him. As if hearing the song for the first time, Ian intently listened to the lyrics as he watched Billy sing. Within seconds, everyone disappeared and it was just the two of them, and Billy was singing the song about a broken road leading directly to him.

He imagined he must have looked like a puppy dog waiting for a pat on the head when Jean whispered into his ear, "Snap out of it, honey."

Startled, Ian said, "Was it that obvious?"

"It's that obvious to me."

"I can't help it, baby cakes. That's some guy up there."

"I'm so glad you think so because I happen to agree."

"Jean, I'm almost ashamed to say it, but I'm mesmerized by him. Not only is he the most genuine man I've ever met, but as an entertainer he has this rare ability to take hold of his audience and never let them go. Me included, and I've been doing this for how long now? I thought I was immune to such things."

"He does have that special something that resonates with the audience," Jean said.

"It's really magical the way he connects with them on every level."

"Oh, Ian. You sound like you've got it bad," Jean said with a smile.

"Help me! Please!" Ian said, laughing, as he shifted his position.

"How's the ankle, honey?"

"It's fine. I just need to stay off of it for another day or two. Then it will be all better."

"That's good. How about another beer? Oh, and by the way, I saw Josh and Suzie at the bar earlier. Did you have anything to do with that?"

"Maybe a little," Ian said with a sheepish grin.

"I thought so. I'll be right back."

In just under an hour, Billy was singing his last song and the crowd was screaming their appreciation. Whistles and cheers and stomping told the band he was up for one more. He once again sat center stage with his guitar and a single spot and closed his set with "The Love of a Man." He hit every note perfectly, just as he'd done the first time Ian had heard him sing it, and sang every word with

124

the sincerity with which he had written them. Billy was a star, Ian recognized; he might not be famous yet, but he was, without a doubt, a star. Billy introduced Jed and hopped off the stage at the same spot he had taken it. Then he headed for Ian.

Jean came back to the table with a beer for Ian and Billy and a Jack Daniels and 7 Up for herself as Billy made his way through the crowd. When he finally made it to the table, he gave Jean a hug. Then he placed his hand on Ian's shoulder and gently squeezed a few times as Ian had done to him before Billy went on stage. It seemed a good way to convey caring that they couldn't otherwise physically express in public. In response, Ian gave Billy a tender look to assure him that he understood.

Billy pulled out a stool for Jean and they both sat. As the three of them chatted about the show, people occasionally interrupted to congratulate Billy, and Ian became a little concerned that Josh and Suzie hadn't made an appearance at the table. He looked around casually so Billy wouldn't pick up on it, but they were nowhere to be seen.

Jean excused herself from the table and Billy leaned over to Ian. "It's okay, handsome. Don't worry about it," he said with a melancholy tone in his voice.

"What do you mean?" Ian said.

"I've noticed you looking around, and I assume it's for Josh and Suzie. Maybe something came up and they'll show up another night."

Before Ian could catch himself, the words flew out of his mouth. "No, they were here."

"Oh," Billy said. "I guess I'm not what he's looking for, then. You said you couldn't guarantee anything and I totally understand that. What means the most to me is that you went out on a limb for me."

"Billy, just because Josh didn't come to the table doesn't mean he didn't like you," Ian said. He wasn't able to keep some apprehension out of his voice.

"Time will tell," Billy muttered. "Let's get you home."

They said their good-byes to Jean and left the saloon. They drove home hand in hand, mostly in silence. When Billy did speak,

125

Ian could hear the disappointment in his voice. He wanted to kick himself for telling Billy that Josh was even coming. How could he have been so stupid?

And the more he thought about it, the angrier he got at Josh. It was just plain rude not to make an appearance at the table, whether he liked Billy or not.

When they got home, Billy went around to the passenger side to help Ian out of the car. He took Ian's crutches from the backseat and threw them in the corner of the garage. Before Ian could slide down from the seat of the SUV, Billy picked him up and started for the stairs. Sensing that Billy needed this, Ian didn't protest but held Billy close as the two men made their way up the stairs.

When they reached the living room, Billy put Ian down on the couch. "How about a glass of wine?" he asked through a slight smile.

"That would be great."

Billy went to the kitchen, poured two glasses of wine, and sat down next to Ian. Ian placed his glass of wine on the table and told Billy to lie back and put his feet up. He did as he was told, and Ian removed both of Billy's boots and began to rub his feet. One foot at a time, Ian kneaded the bottom with his thumbs, trying for all the right pressure points, hoping that some pleasure might replace a little of the disappointment he was experiencing.

When Ian finished, Billy said, "Thank you, Ian."

"No thanks needed. It was my pleasure."

"And I apologize for being such a baby. Even I can't believe how ungrateful I'm acting," Billy said. "I have this incredible opportunity at Jean's and the crowd seems to like what I do, and most importantly, I have you in my life. I don't need any more than that."

Ian felt a lump in his throat. He bent down and kissed Billy on the top of his foot and said, "You're not being a baby. And thanks."

They were about to go upstairs to bed when Ian's phone, which was lying on the couch between them, lit up with a voice mail notification. He and Billy both looked down to see the voice mail was from Josh.

"A message from Josh," Billy said. "I want to hear."

126

Ian froze. He was sure Billy saw the fear on his face, but Billy had a right to hear whatever Josh's message said. The problem was that Josh wouldn't be thinking Billy was going to hear this, so he would be brutally honest. *Oh God, let this be good!* was his last thought as he pressed the speaker and they listened to the message together.

"Ian, hey. I'm sorry we didn't get the chance to come to the table or meet Billy tonight, but we got a call from our babysitter that the baby was running a fever, so we wanted to get home as soon as we could. Anyway, Billy is fantastic; I can't believe no label has signed him yet. Of course we need to follow proper channels, but I think he would be an asset to Capitol. I'll call you tomorrow. Good job."

Billy's eyes were wide as saucers, and Ian was sure *he* was white as a ghost, but he didn't care. Billy was a hit. Billy took both of Ian's hands and pulled Ian up to him, smothering him with slow and passionate kisses.

AFTER A night of celebration, the alarm clock sounded very early. Billy kissed Ian on the neck, climbed out of bed, and headed for the shower. While he washed he mentally ran through the events of last night. Could this be the big break he needed? Could Ian and Josh pull this off? Was he good enough? He hated to go to the ranch with his career hanging in the balance, but he'd made a commitment to the Lazy H and wouldn't go back on his word.

When Billy stepped out of the shower, Ian was there with a fresh cup of coffee. "Morning, cowboy."

"Morning! What are you doing out of bed?"

"I couldn't go back to sleep. I'm too excited. At one minute past nine o'clock, I'll be on the phone with Josh to see how we're gonna handle my new discovery."

"Your new discovery, huh?" Billy teased. "I like the sound of that, even though you make it sound like you found Noah's Ark or something."

"Ha-ha," Ian said. "There's a hell of a lot to do. We've got to pick your first single. We've got to decide which markets to go after

127

first. We've got to find a Capitol artist who's scheduled to go on tour about the time we release your first single to make you an opening act. In addition, we've got to listen to hundreds of demos to choose songs for your first album. Like I said, so much to do."

"Hold on there, pilgrim," Billy protested. "This is not a done deal yet, remember?"

"Technicalities," Ian said. "It's all just formalities. You better get used to the idea that you're going to be a superstar."

Billy stood there dripping wet and lunged for Ian. Ian stepped back just in time to avoid Billy's advance, but reached for a towel and threw it in his direction.

"You escaped this time," Billy said, "but don't expect to escape next time."

"I don't know. I'm pretty fast when I need to be," Ian responded. "Even lame."

"Yeah, but I'm a superstar, and I'm supposed to get everything I want… and right now, I want you. So get over here."

TWENTY MINUTES later Billy was pulling out of the driveway, and Ian was in his office writing down ideas and making notes for his call to Josh. Within minutes the phone was ringing. Ian glanced at the caller ID and saw that it was Billy's cell phone.

"Billy? Is everything all right?"

"Is this all real, Ian?"

"It's very real, Billy."

"Okay. Just checking. I'll call you at the lunch break. But if you hear anything I need to know, you'll call me, right?"

"Will do," Ian promised. "Have a great day."

Ten minutes after nine Ian was on the phone with Josh. He sang Billy's praises for nearly an hour until Josh finally stopped him. "Okay," Josh said. "Stop selling him. I'm already hooked."

"Sorry," Ian said. "I just haven't seen this kind of talent in years."

Josh agreed, and they got down to business: talking strategies, markets, and contracts, making a to-do list with each of them taking away items to complete.

His first task, Josh said, would be to put together an A-list of musicians and schedule the studio time needed to cut a demo, while Ian lined up a Capitol publicist and started working on a preliminary marketing plan. Josh also agreed to get the label execs to Jean's over the next few nights to see Billy perform live as that would make the most impact. Why some other label hadn't signed him already, Josh claimed he couldn't fathom, so he didn't want to waste any time. If a competitor got wind of Capitol's interest in Billy, they would be all over him.

Secretly, Ian hoped that would happen because that's how Billy would get the best deal, but Ian was under a blanket nondisclosure and noncompete agreement with Capitol. Although he wanted to do the best by Billy, he wouldn't risk his job by playing both sides, and he knew Billy wouldn't want that, anyway.

Josh and Ian hung up the telephone. Although Ian couldn't wait to get to work, he'd promised Billy that he would call him if he heard anything, so he kept his promise and punched in Billy's cell phone number.

"This is Billy."

"How's it hanging, cowboy?"

"Uh, a little to the right, but you already know that," Billy teased. "Is everything all right, Ian?"

"I just got off the phone with Josh."

Billy didn't respond.

"Cowboy?"

"Please tell me you've got good news," Billy said hesitantly.

"I've got good news," Ian repeated. "But I can't talk now. I've got work to do."

"Very funny," Billy said nervously. "Tell me, pleeeease."

"I think I like it when you beg," Ian whispered.

"Please stop teasing me and tell me what's going on," Billy said, sounding defeated.

"Okay, okay. I spent the last couple of hours on the phone with Josh, and he's very excited about you. He's handpicking musicians and scheduling studio time for a demo."

"Are you serious?"

"Very serious," Ian replied. "I'm about to get on the phone with a Capitol publicist and start on a preliminary marketing plan. And cowboy?"

"Yeah?" Billy said.

"You better start thinking about giving notice at the Lazy H. Your life is about to get very complicated."

"I can't believe this is happening," Billy mumbled.

"And it's only the beginning," Ian said.

"I don't know what to say. Thank you, Ian."

"It's all you, Billy. Now let me get back to work and call me on your way home."

Chapter Fifteen

THE ENTIRE next month was a blur to Billy. Billy, Ian, and Josh spent time in the recording studio with some of the best musicians Billy had ever worked with. They recorded two demos: a cover of "Moments" by Emerson Drive, which Billy had sung the night he'd won the open mic contest, and "The Love of a Man," which he always used as an encore at Jean's.

While Billy was still performing at Jean's, Ian was entertaining various label executives, who stopped in to see what all the hoopla was about. When he and Ian were at home, Ian was on the phone constantly with Capitol's public relations and marketing departments and Billy's new publicist, making plans for Billy's launch.

Billy spent endless hours with an attorney Jean had recommended to help negotiate the contract, and although Ian was already under an employment contract with Capitol, he helped guide Billy in the right direction.

Two weeks prior to the date he was to sign the recording contract, Billy gave his notice at the Lazy H Ranch.

Before he knew it, he was saying his good-byes to the guys at the ranch, all of them vowing to keep in touch and telling him to remember that they knew him when.

In preparation for leaving the ranch, Billy had to find a place to live. He knew it was too soon to talk about sharing Ian's townhouse permanently, not that Ian had extended the invitation. But even if Ian had made the offer, Billy knew he should have his own place in case it ever came up with the press. So he did some hunting and found a great little one-bedroom right off Broadway, near Jean's. He also figured that it wouldn't hurt to have a place downtown if he and Ian had a late night in Nashville and didn't want to make the hour drive back to Westhaven. It seemed like everything was falling into place. He and his attorney had negotiated what he thought was a great recording contract; he had a roof over his head, in fact two roofs; and most importantly, he had Ian. His life was moving right along as scheduled.

On the morning Billy was to sign his recording contract, he woke to an empty bed. He could barely catch a hint of coffee through a strong smell of burning bacon. He instantly knew Ian was trying to make him a celebratory breakfast and smiled at the effort. Hopping out of bed, he pulled his jeans on and ran downstairs. As he had pictured it in his mind, there was Ian in front of the stove, cursing and mumbling about burned bacon and rubbery eggs. He walked up behind him and snuggled into his back. "Morning, handsome."

"What are you doing down here, cowboy? I'm trying to surprise you with breakfast in bed, although I'm not doing such a great job."

"Everything looks perfect to me," Billy said. "Let's eat."

"At your own risk," Ian laughed.

"I'll take any risk if it will make you happy."

"Even if you end up in the hospital and miss the signing of your new recording contract?"

"You've got a good point. You try it first."

"Very funny," Ian said.

"I'm just kidding. It looks perfect, and besides," Billy replied, "I'm so hungry I could eat anything."

"Oh really? But just so you'll know, that kind of backward compliment will get you everywhere."

"I'll remember that," Billy said.

They finished breakfast, and it wasn't half-bad. Billy thought Ian's cooking was getting better, but he also thought it was best that he continue his role as head chef, just for their safety. Ian rinsed the dishes, and Billy loaded the dishwasher, and when they were finished, they went upstairs to get showered and dressed for the big day.

Traffic was pretty light, so they made good time. They pulled into the parking garage at Capitol with thirty minutes to spare. When they reached the glass-enclosed conference room, Josh was already there, as were Billy's attorney and two other attorneys representing Capitol.

Josh said, "Morning, boys. Since we're all here, do you want to get started?"

"Morning, Josh," Ian said, and he nodded to the attorneys.

"Morning, all." Billy and Ian exchanged smiles, and Billy said, "Let's get this show on the road."

Ian sat fairly silently as the attorneys shuffled papers back and forth and handed them first to Billy for his signature and then to Josh for his. The entire process took less than an hour, and before noon, Billy Eagan was Capitol Records Nashville's latest recording artist.

When the process was complete, they all took turns shaking hands and congratulating Billy. As a tradition, Josh always took his new talent to a celebratory lunch or dinner, depending on the time, at Tootsie's Orchid Lounge. Tootsie's was well known in Nashville, steeped in country music history and guaranteed to provide a glimpse of country music's finest. Since Josh and Ian pretty much knew everyone in Nashville, as soon as they walked in, Ian got a wave from Troy Gentry, of Montgomery Gentry, sitting in the corner with his wife. Josh headed over to a table of three men. One was Capitol producer Scott Hendricks and the other two were Luke Bryan and Chris Cagle. Josh waved Ian and Billy over, and Ian said his hellos and introduced Billy to the three men. "So you're the guy we've been hearing so much about," Scott said.

Billy blushed and said, "I don't know about that, but I'm very excited to meet you guys. I love your work."

"Thanks, man," Chris said.

Luke nodded and said, "Yeah, thanks. Welcome aboard."

"Hopefully we'll be able to work together soon," Scott said.

"I'd like that," Billy responded.

As the three men left the table, Josh and Ian explained that Scott had just produced Chris's new album and was about to do one for Luke, so he was a good man to know. They walked back to the hostess and were seated at a table across from the popular "window booth," usually reserved for paying tourists who wanted to sit where famous people like Willie Nelson, Waylon Jennings, and Kris Kristofferson enjoyed some downtime.

After they ordered their lunch, Josh said, "Billy, your life is about to become pretty demanding."

"Nothing I can't handle," Billy said. "I've waited for this all of my life, and I won't let a bunch of demands do me in."

"Great attitude," Josh said. "And besides, Ian will be there to make sure you don't screw this up."

Billy and Ian exchanged glances like guilty six-year-olds caught with their hands in the cookie jar. *I wonder if he suspects that Billy and I are more than friends?* Ian had never come out to Josh or anyone at work; there was never a need. He'd been able to dodge the "fix me up" game by always working and traveling a good bit, so eventually people gave up and stopped trying. Ian snapped back to reality and straightened in his chair.

"Josh, since you brought up the fact that I will be right there with Billy, I've been considering something for a while now and wanted to talk to you about it. In fact, Billy doesn't even know what I'm about to say, so you're both hearing it for the first time."

Billy raised an eyebrow, and Josh looked at Ian expectantly.

Ian cleared his throat. "Josh, you already know I found Billy and brought him to Capitol, and you also know that I've taken a personal interest in his career and getting him signed. And, well, to be honest, we work really well together and, well, I wanted to know… wondered if you'd have a problem with me focusing on his career full time?"

134

Josh's mouth dropped open. "You want to leave Capitol and manage Billy's career?"

"Yes and no. I would prefer not to leave Capitol, but I do want to manage his career."

Billy's eyes widened. He smiled and looked at Josh and asked, "Could that happen?"

"Technically, yes," Josh said, "but Capitol's management division only handles their top-tier talent and only if it makes a hell of a lot of sense to keep it in-house."

Ian defended his idea. "Before you rule it out, I'm prepared to leave Capitol and go out on my own if that's what it takes, but I would certainly rather have the Capitol machine behind me."

"Now, wait a minute, Ian," Billy said, taking his turn at sitting up straight. "You're not going to quit your job to take a chance on me."

"Listen to the man," Josh said to Ian.

"Too late, boys, my mind's made up," Ian said. "And besides, the label knows what they have in Billy or they wouldn't have signed him so quickly. I think they would prefer to have some control over his career, beyond his contractual obligations. By allowing me to manage him, they get the best of both worlds. Think about it, Josh. If Billy hires an outside manager, his or her loyalty would lie with Billy alone, not the label. And you know from past experience that could get ugly. If they allow me to do it under the Capitol umbrella, I, of course, would do what's best for Billy, but I would do it with Capitol's best interests in mind as well."

Josh looked at Ian, then in Billy's direction, and finally back at Ian. "Let me think about this for a day or two and run it by a couple of people to get a sense of general consensus," he said. "Billy's an unproven artist, and that's a pretty big risk for the label."

"No problem," Ian said, "but Capitol knows my track record, and they know I can do this, so don't wait too long. I know we have something great with Billy, and the label knows that too."

"Okay" was the last thing Josh said as he stood, shook Billy's hand, affectionately smacked Ian on the back of the head, and left the table.

"Where in the hell did that come from?" Billy asked, cocking his head to one side and glaring at Ian.

"Don't give me that look; just hear me out. I've had this in the back of my mind since our first meeting at Jean's. I've seen new artists get signed just to have their manager clash with the label and get released from their contract in a flash. The best way I know how to guarantee your success is to manage you myself. I know enough people in Nashville and have enough contacts to make this happen. Besides, my reputation is really good, so I'm told. Right now, Josh has his Capitol hat on, and he's playing the game, but he knows it's the best thing for everyone. He's a smart man. He'll make it happen."

Billy and Ian downed their iced tea and left right after Josh. Since Billy was performing at Jean's later that night and they had an early meeting at Capitol the next morning, they drove in the direction of Billy's apartment.

"Hey, cowboy," Ian said.

"Yes, handsome?"

"I don't know if you know this, but the Country Music Awards are next week."

"Of course I know that. What about it?"

"I was wondering if you could help me find a date."

"Does this date have to be a woman?" Billy asked sarcastically.

"I usually take Jean, but this year I was thinking I wanted to switch it up a bit."

"How much of a switch?" Billy asked.

"Well, let's see, maybe someone with a penis. Do you know anyone?"

"Yeah, I have one in mind," Billy said.

"Do you think he might be interested in going with me?"

Billy rose up in his seat and said, "Hell, yes." Then he caught himself, leaned back in his seat, and said very calmly, "Um, I mean, sure, he might be interested."

"Oh, he might, huh? What will it take to persuade him? A new dress, maybe?" Ian asked.

"Throw in shoes and a matching handbag, and you've got a deal," Billy said, laughing.

"It's a date, then?" Ian asked.

"It's a date," Billy responded.

Chapter Sixteen

THE NEXT few days after the signing were mostly spent in marketing meetings, planning the release of Billy's first album. They were trying to coordinate the timing of the release so Billy could open for Luke Bryan on his next scheduled tour. That gave them a little over six months to execute the marketing plan.

They had to come up with a name for the album, select and record all the songs, choose the first single, design artwork for CD covers and posters, do photo shoots, write bios and press releases, and book some small gigs to get the buzz out. After much deliberation, they decided to go for it, and the plan was put in motion.

The next week was the CMAs. Ian and Billy made their way down the red carpet with Ian saying hello to everyone he knew and introducing Billy as Capitol's latest artist. When they heard the "five minutes until live" warning, they headed for their seats. Because of Ian's position with Capitol and the fact that Billy was a new recording artist, they were fifth row, center.

Billy and Ian found their seats, and right before they sat, Billy placed his hand on Ian's shoulder, smiled, and squeezed three times. Ian smiled back.

Everywhere Billy looked, he saw a celebrity. When he looked to the left, he saw Reba McIntyre, Keith Urban, George Strait, Tim McGraw, and Faith Hill. He looked to the right and saw Kenny Chesney, David Nail, Scotty McCreery, and Ronnie Dunn. On his same row, a few seats down, were Josh and Suzie Randal, along with some of his fellow Capitol artists: Luke Bryan, Dierks Bentley, Darius Rucker, and Eric Church.

Billy couldn't believe he was there. This was big time, and he was eating it up. After the awards show, they went to the Capitol Records party, and Ian introduced Billy to as many celebrities as he could. He was doing his job, and his job right now was getting Billy's name out there.

Ian was very impressed that Billy stayed cool, calm, and collected on the surface, when all the while he knew on the inside he was terribly starstruck. When the night finally ended, Billy was walking on air. He felt like Cinderella at the ball, and Ian was there to share this first big event with him.

Eventually, Capitol came through and allowed Ian to manage Billy's career. Within days, the Capitol Records Nashville marketing machine was moving full speed ahead, with no slowdown in sight. After the first month, Billy realized that he'd really had no clue what Josh had meant when he'd said his life was about to become very demanding.

The merry-go-round started to spin faster and faster, and he held on for the ride. The first few weeks had been spent selecting songs for the first album. "The Love of a Man" was chosen as his first single, which made Billy very happy, and since they had already recorded it as a demo, they laid down an additional instrumental track, and it was ready to go. They planned to release it in thirty days and let the momentum build while he recorded the rest of the album. Next came the photo shoots, interviews with Nashville radio stations, more shows at Jean's—this time as a headliner—small three-day tours in the surrounding area, and lastly, wherever an event took place around Nashville, Ian had him there, smiling and singing.

The morning of the release, Ian and Billy woke at five o'clock to the sound of George Strait singing "River of Love" on Billy's alarm clock. Billy had performed at Jean's the night before while Ian stayed behind at Billy's apartment, tweaking the final press release. Billy moaned as Ian broke free from his embrace, rolled over, and turned off the alarm clock.

Ian jumped out of bed and made a dash for his laptop computer, then quickly slipped back into the bed when Billy held up the covers as an invitation. He snuggled back against Billy while the computer hummed and clicked to life. Billy softly brushed his mouth against Ian's lips. Ian's faint whimper was all the response Billy needed. The kiss they exchanged was dreamy and heated, filled with lust and desire. But when the computer finished the booting process, Ian said, "Slow down, cowboy. We've got work to do."

"Damn," Billy said, "I was just getting started."

"That's what I was afraid of," Ian retorted. "But don't worry, I'll make it up to you later."

Ian opened his e-mail program and quickly scanned his inbox. He found the e-mail he was looking for from the PR department and double-clicked on it to read the contents. Billy's press release had crossed the newswire at 4:35 a.m. Ian wanted the release out early so the morning radio shows would get it before they began to broadcast, which was usually around five thirty. He then logged on to the Internet and went to CMT's website. He went directly to the "Press" section, and within seconds he had Billy's press release in front of him. The heading read "Capitol Nashville Recording Artist Billy Eagan Releases First Single."

Ian had already confirmed that hundreds of CDs containing the song had been sent out the previous week, as scheduled, to every country music radio station in the United States and Canada, with an embargo date to coincide with the press release. The embargo date guaranteed that the song wouldn't get any airplay until the press release hit the wire. "Well, cowboy, if I've done my job right, and I think I have, within a day or two, with some luck, we should start hearing you on the airwaves."

Billy yawned and said, "I'm always so amazed at how effortlessly you do your job. This all comes so easily to you, like second nature."

"Like any job, when you do it enough, it does become second nature. I imagine like singing is second nature to you," Ian responded, with a yawn of his own.

140

Billy took the laptop out of Ian's hands, placed it on the floor, reached over, turned the clock radio on this time, and said, "Just in case. Now. Where were we?"

"Just about to take a shower," Ian said. "We have the first of seven interviews in just about an hour at 97.9 WSIX, and they asked us to do a few sound bites and promos before the interview, so we've got to get a move on."

"This new career is putting a serious crimp in my love life," Billy whined.

Ian got out of bed, shaking his head and laughing as he walked into the bathroom and turned on the shower.

The day was as busy as they had all been over the past few weeks: visiting one radio station after another, doing interviews, recording sound bites, taking pictures, and signing autographs. Then off to the next station for more of the same. Billy didn't mind the PR, and in fact, he really liked meeting people and signing autographs, but by the day's end, he thought he would be saying, "This is Billy Eagan, and you're listening to WSIX, 97.9, Big 98 Country" in his sleep.

LATER THAT night was the release party. Billy was to do a short show and a dozen or so press interviews and take as many photos as possible for the Capitol website. The evening went off without a hitch, and when the party ended at a little past midnight, they got into Ian's SUV and drove to Atlanta to repeat the radio station tours and a one-nighter at Miss Kitty's Saloon. The band didn't have to be in Atlanta until four o'clock the next afternoon, so they were leaving in the morning, but Billy and Ian had their first interview at seven o'clock the next morning and one every hour, on the hour, for the other three country stations in the Atlanta area. To help them stay awake, they listened to every country radio station from Nashville to Atlanta, hoping to hear Billy. When the reception started to fade on one radio station, Ian hit the Scan button and stopped it on the next country station. They heard "This is Trisha Yearwood and you're listening to KICKS 101.5," and Billy said, "I know how you feel, honey." Ian chuckled.

"Is it a bad sign that I'm not getting any airplay yet?" Billy asked.

"No, not really. Sometimes it takes a few days, but I can guarantee you that when we're done with the press tours, you'll be sick of hearing yourself on the radio."

It was four thirty in the morning, and they still had a two-and-a-half-hour stretch on I-75 from Chattanooga to Atlanta. Billy had been driving Ian's SUV for almost four hours, and he was starting to get a little fidgety. He was about to press the Scan button to look for another country station when he heard the DJ say, "Don't miss Cadillac Jack in the morning when Capitol Records Nashville recording artist Billy Eagan stops by to talk about his new single and hopefully give us a live performance. But in the meantime, here's Billy Eagan with 'The Love of a Man.'"

"Ian, do you hear that? I'm on the radio. I'm on the frickin' radio!"

"Yeah, cowboy, you are, and if I may say so myself, you sound good enough to eat."

Billy was so excited he pulled across three lanes of traffic and onto the shoulder of the road. He got out of the car, ran around to Ian's door, opened it, and pulled him out. He took Ian into his arms, kissed him deeply in the darkness, and then lifted him into the air and spun him around.

"Thank you, Ian, thank you so much."

"Don't thank me, cowboy; you're the one singing on the radio. Now put me down before we get shot by some drunken redneck."

Billy trembled with excitement. He had no idea hearing himself on the radio would have such an effect on him.

"Billy, get in the car, and I'll drive the rest of the way until you calm down."

"Okay, good idea," Billy said. "I don't want to kill us the same day I hear myself on the radio for the first time. It wouldn't be good karma."

Ian got in the driver's seat and slowly pulled back onto I-75. "What do you know about karma, anyway?"

"For starters, since I met you, I've got a record deal, I've got a newly released single, I'm on the way to do a radio interview and a show promoting my single, and I've got a boyfriend. That sounds like pretty good karma to me."

"Wow, that's a mouthful, Billy. I can't take all the credit. If you didn't have talent, I couldn't have done any of this. I think we make a pretty good team, but no labels as far as we go."

"Gotcha, but speaking of mouthfuls," Billy said with a smile on his face, "I'm about to get me one."

Billy reached over with his left hand and started rubbing Ian's dick through his jeans, and right on cue, it responded.

"Billy, we can't do this here. What if someone sees us?"

"Who's going to see us in the dark?" Billy said while continuing to stroke Ian's now semierect cock. "Maybe a trucker or two, but even if some trucker does see us, my face will be buried in your crotch so deep that no one will be able to see it."

"How can I argue with that logic?" Ian asked. "I really don't want to anyway. Go for it."

Billy unbuttoned Ian's jeans, and Ian lifted up so he could slide them down to his knees, just far enough to get at what he wanted. Ian's now fully erect dick pushed tightly against his Calvin Kleins. Billy opened the fly of Ian's underwear, and his cock popped out and stood at attention. Billy teased Ian's dick by kissing it and circling his tongue around the head several times, then kissing it again. Ian moaned with pleasure and caressed Billy's head and neck. Still teasing the head of Ian's dick, Billy began to suck and nibble while alternating the circular motion.

In one gulp, Billy took the head of Ian's cock to the back of his throat as if attempting to swallow him whole.

Ian moaned, "Yes, cowboy," with delight as he began to move up and down, slowly fucking Billy's mouth.

With his mouth still paying special attention to the top half of Ian's cock and his left hand around the base, Billy attempted to stretch open the fly in Ian's underwear far enough to get at his balls. When the opening was stretched as far as it would go without ripping, he pushed Ian's balls up to meet his mouth. He released Ian's dick momentarily, sucked both balls into his mouth, and tenderly tousled them around until Ian was gyrating in the driver's seat.

Billy released Ian's balls and switched his attention to Ian's rock-hard cock again. He released Ian's dick long enough to stick his middle finger in his mouth and wet it thoroughly, then went back to bobbing up and down while he slipped his hand up the inside right leg of Ian's underwear. Billy found what he was looking for in seconds and felt the tight pucker against his finger. He massaged the opening while continuing to swallow Ian whole and then move up, go down, and swallow again.

Ian said, "Cowboy, I'm about to—" and Billy pushed his finger in Ian's ass as far as it would go. He felt Ian's ass tighten and release around his finger as he bucked, each shot of his load hitting the back of Billy's throat. When Ian was through emptying his balls, Billy slid his finger out of Ian's ass and heard him gasp.

Billy bled Ian dry of every drop of come and saliva, and once convinced he had finished the job, he slid Ian's now soft dick back inside his underwear. Ian lifted again, and Billy pulled his jeans back up to his waist. With one knee on the steering wheel, Ian used both hands to button his jeans.

Leaning back in his seat with his left hand resting on Ian's right leg, Billy closed his eyes and said, "That's the first time I've ever done that, and it was damn hot."

"If this means that every time you hear your song on the radio, I get one of these, cowboy, I'm about to start working a hell of a lot harder."

"I think that's a plan, so get to work."

IAN PULLED off at the next exit for a quick bathroom break. They each got a cup of coffee and a bagel at a drive-through and then got back on the road. They had just enough time to check into their hotel, take a quick shower, and get to the radio station by seven o'clock.

144

By noon they were finished with Billy's interviews and driving back to the hotel to get some rest before the show. They had sound checks at seven o'clock and the show started at ten thirty.

When they got back to the hotel, Billy lay down on the bed and Ian went into the bathroom. When Ian came out, Billy was curled into a ball, fast asleep. Ian tried to remove Billy's boots without waking him, but that was impossible. Then Billy rolled over onto his back, and Ian was able to remove his boots and his jeans. He sat up briefly, and Ian took off his shirt. Billy slipped under the covers while he watched Ian undress. Ian set the alarm for six o'clock to be ready for the seven o'clock sound check, after which they could come back to the hotel, shower, and get a bite to eat before the show.

Satisfied that all bases were covered, Ian slipped under the covers with Billy and closed his eyes. Billy lay still for a few more minutes, and just as Ian was sure he was asleep again, he turned, snuggled up behind Ian, and said, "I love you, Ian."

Ian wasn't asleep, and the words Billy murmured repeated in his head over and over.

THE NEXT six months were more of the same: press junkets, radio interviews, and one-nighters, but they were all paying off because Billy's single was at number fifteen on the country-music charts and climbing.

The album was finally finished and the release was scheduled in two weeks, to coincide with the kickoff of Luke and Billy's tour. Billy and Ian had the last week before the tour to rest. They'd planned on going down to New Orleans for a few days, since Ian had never been there and Billy didn't know when he would have time off again to visit his family.

But before their vacation, they had to get through Nashville's Fanfare, an event sponsored by all the record labels and designed to let fans get up close and personal with the artists. Billy had endless hours of meet and greets with his growing fan base, posing for photos and signing autographs, and he thoroughly enjoyed every minute of it.

Luke was performing on the last night to officially close the event, and Ian arranged to have Billy open for him to test the lineup for the tour. It was Billy's first big concert, and he was ready for it. He was a sensation. The crowd loved him, the label execs loved him, Luke loved him, and as Ian stood in the wings watching Billy finish his encore, he knew in that very moment that he, too, loved Billy. Not just loved him but was in love with him.

The realization hit him hard, and he stood there frozen with his eyes closed, on the verge of tears—not tears of happiness, but tears of fear and panic. *This wasn't supposed to happen. How could this have happened? I was careful, wasn't I? I kept everything in proper compartments. Didn't I?*

He had convinced himself that he was only along for the ride. Just there to get Billy where he needed to be. He could quit anytime and not look back. What was he going to do now?

WHEN BILLY came offstage, he was exhilarated. It was like he was high on something—the fans, the lights, and the energy. It was like he had just performed for the first time.

Where's Ian? he thought. *I need Ian.* People were crowding him, congratulating him, and Josh was there with a huge grin on his face, but no Ian.

"Josh, have you seen Ian?"

"He was here with me during the encore, but then he said he wasn't feeling too well and went back to your trailer."

When Billy finished thanking all the well-wishers, he went straight to his trailer to find Ian. When he opened the door, the trailer was in darkness. He flipped on the lights and realized that Ian had been sitting there in the dark. He ran to his side and saw tears running down Ian's cheeks.

"Ian, what's wrong, are you sick? Should I call a doctor?" No response. "Ian, talk to me."

"I'm fine. I just need to go home."

"Okay, I'll have you home in fifteen minutes. Let's go," Billy said.

"No, I want to go to my house in Westhaven," Ian replied.

"Sure, whatever you want, but can I ask why?"

"We need to talk," Ian said.

"About what?" Billy asked with panic in his voice.

"Not here" was all Ian said.

THEY DROVE to Westhaven in silence. Billy tried to get Ian to talk, but it was useless. It was like he'd just shut down. He was cold and distant, not himself, not the Ian he had fallen in love with.

When they got home, Ian walked directly to his bedroom and Billy followed.

"Okay, we're home. Now talk to me."

Ian said, "I can't go on tour with you, Billy."

"Why the hell not?"

"Because I can't. I'll call Josh and have them assign another manager to your career. You'll be fine. Your career has a momentum of its own now. You'll be okay."

"I don't want another manager, Ian. I want you."

"You can't have me, Billy."

"What are you saying, Ian? This is it, just like that?"

"Yes, that's exactly what I'm saying. It's better this way."

"Better for whom?" Billy shot back.

"Better for both of us," Ian said. "Go to New Orleans, go on tour, and enjoy your career. You earned it."

"I don't want any of it without you, Ian. I love you."

"Billy, don't say that. It can't work."

"Ian, you can't push me away. I won't go without a fight. You've got to tell me what happened to you, who hurt you so terribly that you're willing to give up on us. This is killing me, and it's killing you."

Through sobs, Ian said, "It doesn't matter, Billy. I'm damaged goods, and you deserve so much more than I can offer you. You're

147

the best man I know, and I can't continue to hurt you. You need to let me go."

"Don't begin to think you can tell me what I need," Billy said. "I know you give me everything you can, and I've never asked for anything more than that. You wanted no labels and you got no labels. I kept my feelings to myself. Do you know how many times I wanted to tell you I was in love with you, but didn't?"

"That's why it's not fair to you," Ian said. "No one should have to hold back their feelings."

"But why is this happening now?" Billy asked. "I've never pressured you."

"Because I'm in love with you too, dammit, and I can't—I won't—go through this again," Ian shouted.

Billy yelled back, "You're going to have to, because I won't give up without a fight."

"Please, Billy, don't make me relive this. It's not going to change anything."

"Maybe it won't, but I need to know. You're asking me to let go of the most important thing in my life, and it's not fair to make me do that without an explanation."

"If I tell you, will you go and move on with your life?" Ian asked.

"If you open up to me and tell me what happened to you, and when you're through, you still want me to go, I won't fight you. I love you too much to cause you any more pain."

Ian sat on the edge of the bed, dropped his head in his hands, and said, "Okay, Billy, you win."

IAN OPENED his mouth, but it took a couple of attempts before the name came out.

"Todd Slocum was my best friend since elementary school. We were on the wrestling team together in middle school; we joined the swim team together in high school and continued swimming in college; we became roommates when we went away to Bob Jones University. We were both majoring in marketing, with minors in business administration. Todd's mother was from a prominent South Carolina family, and his father was the district attorney of Greenville. My parents were pretty well-off as well. My mother was a stay-at-home mom who did lots of charity work, and my father was a pediatrician. Our families were longtime friends with strong, Christian values.

"Somewhere between our junior and senior year in high school, Todd developed a romantic attraction to me that I was unaware of. Between the fear of losing his best friend and the fact that his Bible-beating parents considered homosexuality the ultimate sin and damned all homosexuals to burn in hell, Todd kept his feelings for me well hidden. But what Todd didn't know was that I was experiencing the same feelings.

"As we went off to college, it became more and more difficult to pretend or ignore the strong attraction we secretly had for one another. One night, early in our freshman year, we'd gone to a frat party. I didn't really drink much in college, so I was always the designated driver. But as usual, by the party's end, Todd was pretty intoxicated.

"I drove us back to our dorm and struggled to get Todd up the stairs and back to our room, as I had done many times before. When we arrived at the door, I propped Todd against it and held him there with one hand as I fished my keys from my pocket with the other. I slid the key into the lock, turned the knob, and because of Todd's weight, the door flew open with a thud. I lost my footing, and with Todd in my arms, we both fell to the floor. I managed to get him to his feet and maneuvered him toward his bed. When we got there, I could no longer support our weight, and I fell to the bed with Todd on top of me.

"I rolled Todd to one side and slid from beneath him. I repositioned him on the bed with his head on his pillow and started to undress him so he could sleep. As I slid Todd's jeans down to his thighs, I suddenly realized that Todd's dick was very hard. I was shocked. I looked up and saw Todd staring down at me from the head of the bed, resting on his elbows. He managed to get to a sitting position, hook me under both arms, and pull me up to him until we were looking into each other's eyes. Before I could react, Todd reached one hand behind my neck, pulled my head to his, and he kissed me hard. I gladly opened to him. He tasted of beer and nachos, but who cared. He was kissing me, and all I wanted to do was get lost in the moment.

"Something jerked me back to reality, and I pulled away. As hard as it was to stop, I couldn't bear to have Todd not remember this in the morning or, even worse, pretend this interlude didn't happen. Secondly, no matter how much I wanted him, I wasn't willing to take advantage of him, not in this condition. His next move took me by surprise; he reached down and pulled my T-shirt over my head. Before I could get my balance, he pulled me down on top of him, and we were again face-to-face, but this time my bare chest was touching his.

"He began to lightly rub my chest and tease my nipples. He looked at me with such desire that I leapt out of his bed. I needed air, needed to breathe, to think. I didn't want to stop, but I didn't want it this way, either.

"Todd made his way off of the bed and reached out to me. His blue jeans were still around his ankles and he stumbled and lunged forward. I caught him just before he hit the floor. I pulled him back to his feet and wrapped my arms around him, and we stood locked in an embrace that neither of us wanted to break, Todd in his boxers and me naked from the waist up. I reluctantly broke away and guided him back to his bed. He stepped out of his jeans, and I pulled back the covers and nudged him down into his bed. I will never forget the look of rejection in his eyes when I left his side and moved to my own bed, to think and eventually sleep.

"The next morning, I awoke with Todd in his boxers sitting at the foot of my bed. The words between us didn't flow easily, but Todd, despite his hangover, wanted to explain and wanted an explanation. He still wore that look of rejection, and it hurt me to the core.

"Finally he said he shouldn't have kissed me last night and that he was sorry. I asked him why he had done it. He looked down at the floor and I saw tears running down his cheeks. I tried to reassure him and told him it was okay, he could tell me anything. In an almost inaudible tone, he told me he was in love with me. Then he looked at me and told me he'd been in love with me for as long as he could remember but just never had the balls to tell me. But after last night, he couldn't hide his feelings for me any longer. I told him I'd had no idea and that he'd done a pretty remarkable job of keeping his feelings hidden.

"Then I told him that I'd been looking for a sign, any sign, for the longest time, and that I'd almost given up on him and I couldn't believe this was happening.

"The words had barely left my mouth when he said he would leave Bob Jones, change schools. Then as if he had just heard me, he said, 'Wait, did you say you've been looking for a sign? What does that mean?'

"I placed a hand on each side of his face, wiped his tears away with my thumbs, and told him it meant that I loved him too, and I was just as scared to show my feelings. I was so afraid of losing him that I would never have made the first move.

"I nearly cried as I told him that I'd waited forever for a moment like we had shared last night. I had dreamed and fantasized about it more times than I cared to admit, but I didn't want him under those circumstances, not with him intoxicated, not without clear heads. More importantly, I couldn't bear the thought of his rejection in the morning if he regretted it or, even worse, pretended it hadn't happened. I couldn't have lived with that!

"Todd took me in his arms and told me that he loved me. As the words came out of his mouth, I wasn't sure if I'd actually heard them or simply imagined them. I thought I might be dreaming. Then I said I loved him too.

"We looked at each other for the first time with the hopes of a future together. Could it really be possible? Could we actually have a real life together?"

"It sounds like you got everything you ever wanted and then some," Billy said. Ian heard the jealousy in his voice.

"Let me finish, Billy. I need to get through this," Ian said softly.

"After we'd both confessed our love, Todd pulled back the covers and crawled into my tiny bed, and we simply held on to each other. He told me we weren't intoxicated now and that we were both of clear minds. Dealing with a small hangover, but still of clear

151

minds. He asked me where I wanted to go from there. We made love for the first time." With a smile on his face, Ian said, "Neither of us had been with another man before and didn't really know what to do, but we figured it out pretty quickly."

Billy smiled, although the expression looked strained.

"We continued our love affair discreetly through the next semester to the following spring break. Neither of us wanted to think about going home, but our parents were expecting us and we had no good excuse to stay at the University.

"Once back home, we knew we would have to be very careful not to let on how we really felt about each other, knowing our parents would pick up on the slightest indication. Looking back, I think our parents had possibly seen something that we hadn't and had always questioned the time we spent together.

"Spring break came, and we headed home and did the best we could to find time and privacy to be together. The night before we were to head back to school, our parents, who were good friends, were having dinner together and asked us to join them. We declined, with the excuse that we needed to finish laundry, pack, and get a good night's sleep so we could get an early start in the morning.

"Soon after our parents had left for dinner, we went upstairs to Todd's room and tried to relax. We were both very tense from trying to deceive our parents and still find time for each other. We stripped out of our clothes and slipped between the sheets and started to make love.

"Just as we were getting into a rhythm, the door opened and Todd's mother walked into the room with his father in tow. The look of hurt and betrayal on their faces was beyond what we could have ever imagined. We knew they wouldn't approve, but we thought they would come around. Todd jumped up and found his underwear and began to speak. His father raised a hand, and Todd stopped. His father yanked me out of bed and told me to get dressed and get out. He told me to never show my face in their house again.

"I did as I was told. I was sure Todd's parents would call mine, but I had hoped to get home to talk to them before they got the call. Unfortunately, when I got home, my parents were waiting for me. They told me how humiliating it was to hear the Slocums tell them things about their son, things that went against everything they believed in, everything they had taught me. They said I made their stomachs turn. They didn't give me a chance to speak; they told me to pack my bags and get out. As far as they were concerned, they no longer had a son, and I could kiss my family and my education good-bye.

"When I tried to explain that Todd and I were in love, my father accused me of being delusional. Then I asked them what the Slocums had told them. As I stood there listening to my father recount the story, I couldn't believe my ears. The Slocums said that they'd caught me raping Todd. They also said, with his hand on the family Bible, Todd had confessed to being blackmailed. He convinced them that I first raped him after a frat party, when he was intoxicated and couldn't defend himself. Then after that, I had threatened to tell his parents he was gay and get him kicked out of school if he didn't continue to have sex with me. They also told my parents that if I left town immediately and never contacted Todd ever again, they wouldn't press any formal charges.

"I really couldn't believe what I was hearing. I remember falling to my knees and pleading. I told them that wasn't the way it happened and begged them to believe me, but they refused. They told me to go and never come back or face prison time. The last thing my father ever said to me was that I was lucky to evade prison, but prison would be nothing like the fires of Hell, and one day, that's where I would end up for eternity."

"Oh my God, Ian," Billy said as he sat down on the bed and surrounded Ian with his arms.

Ian continued, unable to stop his tears from flowing, "My world had fallen apart in less than two hours. All that Todd and I had acknowledged—the love that I thought would last forever—Todd had given it all up to save his damn education and his inheritance. My life was over. I had no family, no education, and about eighteen hundred dollars in my savings account. So I did as I was told. I left my life and my first and only love, vowing never to let anyone have the opportunity to hurt me again."

Billy continued to hold on to Ian until he stood up, breaking the embrace.

"Now you know," said Ian. "Now you understand why I can never trust anyone ever again."

"Ian, that's the most heartbreaking story I have ever heard, and I can't begin to imagine the pain you were in, but I'm not Todd. I would never sell you out; I could never live with myself."

"It doesn't matter, Billy," Ian said. "My mind's made up."

"You can't be serious, Ian. You can't turn your back on me, on us."

"Billy, you promised that if I told you the story and I still wanted you to leave, you would leave. I also remember you once saying that you'd never break a promise to me. I want you to leave."

Ian watched as Billy stood up and walked to the closet. He was moving slowly, as if every step caused him pain. After he filled his leather bag with some of his things, he turned to go, but on the way out, he stopped in front of Ian, put his arms around him, gently kissed his neck, and said, "I love you."

As he approached the doorway, he stopped, turned, and said, "Don't worry about the rest of my things. I'll come by when I know you're not here and pack them up, and I'll leave my key on the kitchen counter." He stepped through and slowly closed the door behind him.

Chapter Seventeen

ALTHOUGH BILLY had closed the door gently, the sound rang through Ian's head like a cannon shot. Billy was gone because he told him to go. He stood at the foot of the bed with tears running down his cheeks. He crawled under the covers, and that's where he stayed.

The next morning he made two phone calls. The first was to Josh.
He answered on the first ring. "Josh Randal."
"Josh, it's Ian."
"Hey, what's up?"
"Can you stop by here, or can we meet somewhere? I need to talk to you."
"Ian, what's wrong?"
"Not over the phone, but I really need to talk to you."
"I'll be there in an hour."
"Okay, the front door will be open. Let yourself in."
"Ian, you're scaring me. Tell me what the hell is going on."
"I'll see you when you get here."
In under an hour, Josh was walking in the front door. Ian was seated behind his desk with a bottle of Scotch and a glass.
"Okay, I'm here. What in the hell is going on?" Josh demanded. "And by the way, you look like hell."
"Thanks," Ian said.
"Well?"
"Josh, I don't know where to start."
"Then start at the beginning."

"Okay, you need to get another manager for Billy's tour."

"What? Are you crazy? Why?"

"Because I can't do it, that's why."

"Why not?"

"Josh, I should have told you this a long time ago, and you have every right to fire me, or worse than that, hate me, but Billy and I were involved romantically."

Stunned, Josh just stared at Ian. "You and Billy. Together?"

Ian nodded.

"Oh, man, that complicates things," Josh said. "Why didn't you tell me you were gay?"

"I never meant to keep it from you. I've never had a relationship in Nashville, not even a date, so it was a nonissue."

"Nonissue for you, maybe, but I thought we were friends."

"We are friends, Josh. That's why you're here now."

"You and Billy," Josh repeated. "What happened?"

"It's not Billy's fault. He is one of the best men I know. Please don't blame him."

"I'm not blaming either one of you. You're both my friends, but what happened?"

"Josh, please don't make me get into it, but I will say that Billy deserves more than I can give him."

"Dammit, Ian, I have a right to know, if not as your friend, then as your boss. If this got out, it could have had a serious impact on Billy's career, not to mention how Capitol would feel about you being involved with a client."

"I know, I know. We were involved before he signed with the label, and I never expected it to get this far."

"But it did, and now you and Billy are through, and you want out of his career. Do you know the position this puts me in with the label?"

Ian said, "Josh, I'm sorry," as tears slid down his face.

"Okay," Josh said, "we'll deal with the label later. Let's take care of you."

"I'll be okay. I just need a couple of days to get myself together. Billy and I were scheduled to have this week off before we left for the tour, but I just need a couple of days."

"Take the week and take care of yourself," Josh said. "I'll make up some excuse at work and find someone else to manage Billy."

He stood up, walked around the desk, and put his arms around Ian. "Ian, what happened? You and Billy were great together, at least as friends."

"Josh, thanks for understanding, but it's a really long story, and I don't have the energy to get into it with you. Maybe someday, but not today. I assume that Billy's going ahead with the trip to New Orleans that we planned, so he'll be back by Friday to go over any last-minute issues before the tour."

"Do you need anything, Ian?"

"Nothing you can give me, Josh. Time is the only thing I need right now, the only thing that will help."

"Call me if you need anything, Ian. Suzie and I are your friends and don't you forget it." Josh turned and headed for the door.

"Thanks, Josh, I really appreciate it."

The next call was to Jean. Ian pressed the Talk button on the phone and started to dial, then hesitated. Jean and Jules were under the impression that he and Billy were going to New Orleans, so they wouldn't be expecting him to be home or at the saloon, and he decided not to make that call after all. He just wasn't ready to get into this with them.

He used up all the energy he had left climbing the stairs and getting into bed. All he could do was lie there and try to figure out how he would put his life back together without Billy. He told himself it was better this way, on his terms, before Billy could hurt him. But that did little to ease the pain.

JOSH HAD driven almost halfway home before he suddenly took the next off-ramp, turned his car around, and headed back to Ian's. He wasn't going to allow Ian to shut him out. They had been friends for

157

too long and had too much history. Ian's happiness was important to him, and so what if he was gay and Billy was gay; they were two of his best friends, and they should be happy. They were so good together. He would talk some sense into Ian and get them back on track.

When Josh pulled into the driveway, the house was in darkness. The front door was still unlocked, so he walked in with a determination to make things better for his friends. After searching downstairs, he headed upstairs. He walked into a dark bedroom and flipped the light on. Startled, Ian sat upright in bed with a confused look on his face.

"Get up," Josh said.

"What in the hell do you think you're doing?" Ian yelled.

"I said get up," Josh yelled back. "*Now.*"

Ian got out of bed and said, "Now what?"

"Downstairs," Josh replied.

Feeling defeated, Ian went downstairs as he was instructed and sat on the couch.

"Now tell me what the hell happened to you that was so bad that you would throw away the best thing that ever happened to you."

Ian snapped, "I said I didn't want to get into it."

"I know what you said, and I'm not accepting it. If you're going to get me into some serious trouble with the label over this, then the least you can do is tell me why."

FOR THE second time in one night, Ian hung his head and told someone he cared for about Todd.

Josh listened with an intensity that Ian found intriguing. He asked questions and held all his comments back until the story was over. Finally, Ian said, "Now do you see why I can't go through with this?"

Josh took a deep breath and said, "I can see why you think you can't go through with this. But Ian, Billy is not Todd. Just because Todd had no backbone, that doesn't mean Billy will follow suit. I know Billy, and he is loyal to a fault. What I can see is him standing

158

up for you until death. I've seen this connection between you two, and until now I never knew what it was. But now I see it all too clearly. It was a strong mutual love and support that worked so well for the two of you. Somehow, I sensed that Billy would protect you at all costs, and you would do the same for him. That's why I felt so comfortable going against the label's warnings and pairing you two in business.

"Ian, don't allow your fear to run your life. The worst thing that could happen is that this thing doesn't work out. You got over Todd, and you can get over Billy, but I have the feeling that you will never have to experience that. He loves you, and now I know you love him. Ian, take a chance on Billy. He's a good man and he loves you. He deserves a chance because he's never done anything to make you doubt his loyalty. That's all I have to say, and now I'm going home to the woman I took a chance on, the woman I love and trust with all my heart." Josh turned around and walked out the front door as he'd come in and left Ian sitting on the couch.

Chapter Eighteen

BILLY WALKED out of Ian's house a defeated man. He drove back to town and to his little apartment near Jean's. An hour later he pulled into the parking lot and turned off the ignition, but he couldn't force himself to move. He'd never spent a night there without Ian. How could he enter his apartment without him? His things were still there, Ian's things. Billy put his hand on the door to open it and again hesitated. He thought of Ian, alone and in pain, and that could have easily killed him right then and there if he'd let it.

Sitting in his truck, unable to move, his mind went over and over the events of the night. He was so full of questions and doubt, but in his mind, something didn't add up. His mind brought him immediately to Todd. What could have made him betray Ian in such a horrible way? Ian had said that they were in love and things were going great, so he wasn't looking for an easy way out… or was he? Was Todd as happy as he'd appeared? Ian would have known if he wasn't, wouldn't he? Could Todd have been so scared of his parents and losing his inheritance and education that he'd abandoned Ian emotionally? That didn't sound like the actions of someone in love. Billy thought about what he would have done if he was in that position. He knew the answer without hesitation: he would've told his parents to shove it and he would've been gone. Billy knew the answers he was looking for lay with Todd, and he would be taking a big risk, but he would get his answers. He loved Ian too much to let him go.

Billy took his keys out of the ignition, opened the door of his truck, and, with renewed hope, made his way to his apartment. It ewas as gloomy and heartbreaking as he'd thought it would be, but he fought the urge to stop and give in to the pain in his heart. He proceeded to the bedroom, stopping only long enough to drop his bag of clothes on the bed and move to the computer. Billy knew that if he stopped even for a second and lost sight of his mission, he might just collapse on the bed and never get up. He had to stay focused.

Logging on to the Internet, Billy went to the Google search engine. He typed in "people searches" and reviewed his options. There were many free sites, but he wanted an advancd site that allowed him to enter all the information he knew, which might narrow down his results. He selected a site, and it brought up a full screen of search criteria. Billy typed in Todd's first and last name and Greenville, SC, as his last known address. He knew that each question he was able to answer would significantly narrow his search results, so he thought about everything Ian had told him about Todd. Continuing to enter the search criteria, Billy selected an approximate age of twenty-eight, college graduate of Bob Jones University, single versus married—just a hunch—search area up to two hundred miles surrounding Greenville. And lastly, he clicked the button that signaled the software to provide search results that met all or some of the search criteria. If he got no results, he would expand the search distance until he did get the desired results. He hit the enter key.

As the software's little flashlight moved back and forth, indicating the search was in progress, Billy kept his fingers crossed. He knew his results would present many options, but he hoped it would be manageable. No matter how many names came up, he would call each and every person until he found the right Todd. His and Ian's future depended on it.

When the flashlight stopped, the screen presented seventeen Todd Slocums in the greater Greenville and surrounding areas. After entering his credit card information, the software revealed all the known information about the list of Todd Slocums.

The first four were in Anderson, SC, five were in Spartanburg, SC, two were in Greenville, SC, and six were in Charlotte, NC. Only ten of the seventeen had graduated from Bob Jones, so he was able to eliminate seven prospects. The results had pretty extensive

161

information, like home address and telephone number; employer's name, address and telephone number; spouses, if married, and number of children, etc. Of the ten remaining prospects, one worked for a market research firm and two worked for advertising agencies, and Billy remembered Ian saying that they were both majoring in marketing with minors in business administration. If Todd had followed his major and gone into marketing, that could narrow the search, but if he'd chosen his minor in business administration, that could mean numerous possibilities. While he printed off the list, Billy wondered if someone knew all this information about him, and if so, how in the hell did they get it?

Since it was early evening, he started by calling the home numbers of the two prospects in Greenville. The first call was answered by a woman. Billy asked for Todd, and within seconds a male voice came to the phone.

"Hi, my name is Billy Eagan. I'm looking for a college friend of a friend of mine. Did you happen to know a guy named Ian Dillon while you were at Bob Jones?"

"Um, the name doesn't ring a bell. What did he look like?"

"Well," Billy said, "he's about five ten, blond hair with green eyes, and he was on the swim team."

"No, not that I can recall," Todd said.

Billy knew that when he got the right Todd Slocum, he wouldn't have to think about it. Billy said, "Thanks for your time" and hung up the phone. He called the next Todd Slocum on the list. This time a man answered.

"Hi, is this Todd Slocum?" Billy asked.

"Who's calling?" the male voice replied.

Billy told the man his name and why he was calling, and again, no connection.

The next Todd Slocum on the list lived in Spartanburg and worked for an advertising agency. After a four rings, he got an answering machine and left his name and cell number. Continuing on, the next also lived in Spartanburg and owned a marketing firm. This time a man answered, and when Billy asked if he was Todd Slocum, the male voice said, "Nope, hang on a second." He heard the voice yell, "Todd, pick up the phone," and then someone picked up another telephone extension. The man said, "Hello," and Billy again explained who he was and why he was calling. There was silence on the other end of the line.

Billy said, "Hello?"

"I'm here," Todd said.

"Did you know Ian?" Billy asked again.

"Yeah, I knew Ian," Todd said.

Bingo, Billy thought as he heard Todd sigh on the other end of the phone.

"Todd, Ian needs your help."

"Is he in some kind of trouble?" Todd asked.

"No, nothing like that," Billy replied.

"What, then?" Todd asked.

"It's a long story, and you're a big part of it. Do you have time to talk to me?" Billy asked.

"Ian made his decision concerning me many years ago. I don't know what I can do for him—or you, for that matter. Does he know you were looking for me?"

"No," Billy admitted. "But please, just hear me out."

"You've got five minutes to tell me how and why I should help Ian," Todd said.

"Deal," said Billy. He told Todd how he and Ian had met and how their friendship had grown into a relationship.

"I hope you two will be very happy together, but I still don't know what this has to do with me."

"Please, allow me to finish," Billy said.

He told Todd what had happened earlier that evening between him and Ian and slowly began to recount the story, word for word, as Ian had told it to him. Fifteen minutes later, Billy asked, "Todd, is that what happened? So much doesn't add up to me."

"I can't believe... this can't be true," Todd said in a very shaky voice. "That's not how it happened at all. My parents told me that Ian had blamed me for everything and admitted to them that he was never really into me and had plans to leave town and not return to college. I argued with them for hours that he'd never betray me like that, and when they couldn't convince me of it, they finally told me that they'd paid him twenty thousand dollars to leave town and never see me again. They convinced me that he'd never loved me, and the fact that he accepted the money was surely proof of that."

"Todd," Billy said, "Ian never took any money. Your parents played you both to get what they wanted. They threatened Ian with rape charges if he didn't leave town, with you as their star witness. And they told you that Ian abandoned you for twenty thousand dollars. Todd, if you don't believe me or Ian, maybe it's time you have a talk with your parents."

"I can't," Todd said. "They were both killed in an automobile accident over six years ago."

"I'm sorry, Todd."

"Don't be. We didn't have any real relationship after they discovered that I was gay. They agreed to pay for the remainder of my college if I followed their rules, but once I graduated and they could no longer control me, we broke all ties and never spoke again. I didn't even attend their funeral."

"I can't believe that both of you had to endure such prejudice and hatred from your own parents. Todd, Ian needs to hear the truth, and he needs to hear it from you. I love him dearly, but if he still loves you and there's a chance that you guys could work things out, I love him enough to let him go."

"Billy, Ian and I were over a long time ago. I have someone in my life, for seven years now, who deserves my love and respect. I would never turn my back on him for anyone."

Billy sighed. "I understand and admire your decision, but will you consider making a trip to Nashville? If for nothing else, closure for both of you? Ian is a broken man, and we need to act quickly. I'm very concerned about him."

"Let me talk to my partner and see how he feels about this whole thing, and I'll call you back shortly."

Billy gave Todd his cell phone number, along with his thanks, and ended the call. All he could do now was hope and pray that Todd would help him.

He knew he was taking a big chance. Ian might never forgive him for contacting Todd, but if that was the case, he told himself that if Ian could get some closure, it would be worth it. But in his heart, he believed in Ian and knew that he would eventually understand that Billy couldn't stand by knowing this information and not share it with him. He lay in the darkness of his bedroom, waiting.

Within an hour, Billy's phone rang. He looked at the caller ID and took a deep breath. His phone barely made it to the second ring before he answered it.

"Hello," he said as his voice cracked.

"When do you want to do this?"

"Can you come tomorrow?"

"It's about a six-hour drive. I'll leave early in the morning, and with any luck, I'll be there by eleven," Todd said.

Billy gave him directions to Ian's. "I'll be there to meet you, Todd, and thanks."

Chapter Nineteen

BILLY TRIED to sleep, but it was no use. How was he supposed to rest in the bed he and Ian had shared since he'd moved here? Just then the phone rang, and Billy picked it up immediately, thinking it would be Ian. But to his disappointment, the caller ID said Buck Stevens.

"Hello."

"Billy. I'm so glad you picked up."

"Buck?" Billy said.

"Yeah, it's me. I'm sorry to bother you, but Jules is hurt, and I need help. He won't go to the hospital. Jean is here, and she asked me to call you. We're in the west barn."

"I'm on my way," Billy said without hesitation.

"Thanks, man," Buck shouted into the phone, and then he hung up.

Billy quickly dressed and headed out to the ranch. On the way he tried to call Ian, but the call went straight to voice mail. "Damn, Ian," he said to himself as he left him a voice mail telling him what was going on.

When he arrived at the ranch, everything was quiet. Billy first went to the west barn, but there was no sign of Jules or Jean. Maybe Buck had confused the west and east barns as he had on Billy's initial job interview? Billy ran to the east barn and saw Buck standing just inside the door with a baseball bat in his hand. He didn't have a chance to speak before he went down.

166

JUST BEFORE noon, Todd came to a stop in front of Ian's townhouse. The plantation shutters were all closed and the house was in darkness. Todd discreetly parked his car in front of the neighbor's house and waited for Billy to arrive. He hadn't slept at all worrying about the day's outcome. He kept telling himself that, either way, the truth would come out, and that was all that really mattered.

As he waited he relived the call from Billy. He had sounded so desperate, but all Todd could think about was how all these years he'd thought Ian had abandoned him for money. And how much that had hurt. But that was nothing compared to Ian thinking that Todd had accused him of rape and was going to testify against him if he didn't leave town. At least I got to finish college and keep my family, no matter how awful they were, Todd thought. Ian was forced out of town with no education and no money. Todd couldn't imagine what Ian must have gone through.

When Todd looked at his watch, he realized he'd been sitting there for over an hour. He tried calling the cell phone number Billy had given him, but there was no answer.

What have I gotten myself into? Now what do I do?

He waited about fifteen minutes more, tried calling Billy one more time, and made his decision. Todd walked up the stairs leading to the front door and stood there for a minute, frozen. He willed his arm to reach for the door knocker. When his hand landed on the knocker, he only hesitated a second and then slammed it against the door, over and over.

"THIS BETTER be important," Ian muttered as he opened the door, ready to snarl angrily at the noisy intruder.

His emotion quickly changed from anger to shock and then just as quickly to rage as he recognized the visitor. All the hurt Ian had buried eight years ago instantly rushed to the surface, as fresh and fervent as it had been the day he'd left South Carolina forever. "What the hell are you doing here?" he hissed.

As Todd opened his mouth to speak, Ian tensed. He involuntarily clenched his hand into a tight fist and lifted his arm to strike the intruder from his past.

Todd put his arms in front of his face to protect himself from the damage Ian's blow would surely deliver. "Ian, don't," he yelled. "Billy sent me! Hear me out. Then if you still want to beat me senseless, we'll give it a go."

Ian stared into Todd's eyes, unsure of what to do next. Should he just beat the man to a pulp now or listen to what he had to say and then beat the hell out of him? Exhausted from the emotions of the last two days, Ian relaxed his fists, dropped his arm, and stepped aside as Todd Slocum entered his home.

Ian closed the door behind them. "Say what you need to say and get out. And what does Billy have to do with this?"

"He asked me to come," Todd said. "He loves you."

"Yeah, well," Ian said, "after what you did to me eight years ago, I can't love anyone ever again, so you can thank yourself for whatever I've become."

"No, Ian," Todd said. "My parents played us both."

"What are you talking about?" Ian barked back.

"They told me they offered you twenty thousand dollars to leave town, and you took it, saying you never loved me anyway. And now because of Billy, I know they told you I accused you of raping me. Ian!" Todd said with tears in his eyes. "They played us, man, both of us. I loved you. I could never have accused you of rape. But they spent hours convincing me that you sold me out for twenty grand. And after all, you did leave town."

Shaking his head like he wasn't hearing correctly, Ian stood there, chilled to the bone. He finally muttered, "Yeah, I left town. I had to. They told me if I didn't, they would have me arrested for rape and that you were prepared to testify against me."

Todd moved to Ian's side and took his hand. "I know, man. I know. They lied to both of us."

Tears began to run down Ian's cheeks. He wrapped his arms around Todd. "I loved you too. I would never have left you for any amount of money."

Todd and Ian stared blankly at each other for a moment and then, for the first time in over eight years, held each other tightly. When they broke the embrace, they sat down and talked for almost two hours. Todd told Ian about his relationship with his parents, how they'd died, his career path, and his relationship back home. Ian shared the pain and loneliness he'd felt at the abandonment of his parents, the road to rebuilding his life, about Jean and Jules, and of course, Billy.

"Billy?" Ian said. "Oh my God, I need to talk to Billy."

BILLY WOKE up with the worst headache he had ever experienced in his life. He was lying on a bunk bed with his hands tied over his head and his feet secured to the rails at the foot of the bed. He could feel something sticky on his face and neck, blood he presumed, and he didn't know where he was or how he'd gotten there. The last thing he remembered was going out to the ranch to help Buck. *Buck.* Then he remembered. Buck had struck him with a baseball bat in the barn.

As Billy's eyes slowly adjusted to the dim light, he saw split rails neatly stacked on one side of the room and rolls of barbed wire on the other, and suddenly, he realized where he was. He was in the old cabin they used to store supplies for repairing the many miles of fence surrounding the property. After blinking a few times and scanning the room for any chance of escape, he realized he was not alone in the cabin. There was another bed across the room, and there was someone tied to that bed as well. A woman. His mind was still foggy, but he knew he recognized the woman, though for the life of him, he didn't know from where.

Suddenly it hit him. The unconscious woman tied to the bed across from him was Tina Roth, the woman he'd competed against at the open mic contest. Buck's girlfriend.

"Tina," he whispered. She didn't move.

169

"Tina," he said a little louder. Still no response.

"*Tina*," he yelled.

And she began to moan. Her face appeared to be badly bruised, and she had a black eye.

She was moaning louder now and attempting to move. When she realized her hands and feet were tied to the bed, she began to panic and struggle to get free.

"Tina," Billy said. "Calm down. You can't get loose."

"Who are you?" she screamed. "Help me."

"Tina, it's Billy Eagan. I used to work at the Lazy H ranch, and we competed at open mic night at Jean's. Remember?"

"Oh, Billy," she pleaded. "Help me. Buck's crazy. He beat me up last night because I tried to leave him. He said if I tried to leave again that he would kill me." She was frantic.

"Calm down, Tina," Billy said. "I'm going to get us out of this."

Billy thought for a moment and then spoke. "I understand why he thinks he should be angry at you, but how am I involved in this?"

"He hates you, Billy. Because you're gay, for taking the foreman job at the ranch away from him, and for destroying my big break at Jean's. He has it in his mind that I would have won the open mic contest, and I would have become a huge singing star if it wasn't for you. Billy, he's lost it."

Tina looked down. "I never wanted to sing for a living, but Buck said I was really good, and one day I would be discovered, make us rich, and we wouldn't have to worry about anything ever again. I know I have limited talent. I guess I went along with it because I loved him. People tried to warn me about him. They told me he saw me as his way out, his meal ticket, but I didn't believe them. I trusted him. Billy, I'm so stupid," she whispered.

"You loved him, Tina. Love is not stupid," he said.

"Billy, there's one more thing you should know."

"What?"

"Buck confessed last night that he was in the woods the day your boyfriend was hurt. He followed you guys up the mountain and saw you when you stopped for lunch. He said he was so appalled at what he saw, he went back down the mountain and waited by the stream. When your friend entered the stream, he launched a rock at the horse and spooked her. He told me if I ever told anyone, he would say I was in on it. Billy, I'm so scared. What's he going to do with us?"

"I have no idea what his plans are," Billy said, "but I'm going to get us out of here."

Just then the cabin door opened, and Buck walked in. "Look who's awake," he said with a smirk.

IAN GRABBED his cell phone and quickly dialed Billy's number.

He had so many things to say. He needed Billy. He wanted Billy. He was so sorry not to have trusted in their love. The phone rang once and then went immediately to voice mail.

"Billy, it's Ian. Please call me. Todd's here. Please forgive me. I was so wrong. I'm so sorry. I love you. Please call me back."

Ian ended the call and looked at Todd.

"What if it's too late? What if he's already put me out of his mind? What if he's gone to New Orleans without me? I've got to find him."

Ian tore upstairs and put on a pair of jeans, a T-shirt, and some sneakers. He ran back downstairs and looked frantically for his car keys.

Todd looked at him in alarm. "Wait," he said. "You're not driving like this. I'll take you, and we'll find Billy together."

Ian grabbed Todd and put his arms around his neck, then quickly guided his shoulders toward the door.

"Where do we start looking?" Todd said.

"His apartment downtown is as good a place as any," Ian replied.

Todd drove as fast as he could, most of the time over the speed limit but not so much over as to draw unwanted attention. They arrived at Billy's apartment in just under an hour. When they pulled into the parking lot, even before Todd could bring the car to a stop,

Ian jumped out. He ran up the stairs and used his key to open the front door. "Billy," he shouted.

Billy wasn't there. His half-packed suitcase was on the floor next to the bed, so Ian knew he hadn't left for New Orleans yet.

Ian slapped the palm of his hand against his forehead over and over. "Think, Ian. Think. Where would he go?" Then it hit him. "Jean and Jules, or maybe Josh," he said under his breath.

He lifted his phone to call Jean and saw that he had a voice mail. How had he missed that earlier? He listened to the voice with horror as Billy explained the call from Buck and that Jules was hurt.

Ian dialed Jean and she answered on the first ring. "Ian?"

"Jean, how's Jules? What happened? Is Billy with you?"

"What do you mean 'How's Jules?' He's sitting right here, and he's fine."

"He's not hurt?"

"Ian, what's wrong? You sound frantic."

Ian explained the voice mail he'd received from Billy.

"Here's Jules," Jean said.

"Now just slow down, Ian, and tell me what's going on."

Ian repeated everything to Jules.

"This is not good," Jules said. "I should have fired that bastard when I had the chance. I'm on my way to the ranch."

Jules put Jean back on the phone. "We'll meet you at the ranch, honey. Something is up. I never liked that Buck Stevens."

"Oh, Jean, I've got to find Billy. I've got to get to him."

"Okay, honey, calm down," Jean said. "We'll meet you there."

"Jean, if you see Billy before I get there, tell him I love him, and I was so wrong."

"Okay, honey. I will."

BUCK HAD a fuel can in each hand when he walked in the door. He kicked the door shut, and it closed with a loud thud. "What do we have here?" he said. "Are you ladies awake?"

Tina was the first to speak. "Buck, please let me go. I promise I won't leave you." She glanced at Billy with a pleading look and added, "I love you, Buck."

"You don't love me," Buck shouted. "You want to get as far away from me as you can. And you're gonna get your wish. Can't get any farther."

Billy thought for a second before he spoke. He knew the only chance they had to get out of this was to convince Buck that Tina loved him and that Billy would help her make it in the business.

"Buck, what's this all about?"

"You know exactly what this is about, you little queer." Billy could see the hate in Buck's eyes. "All you sick queers do is please yourselves. You take whatever it is you want at the time. Do you worry about anyone else? Hell no. Well, the buck, so to speak, stops here, Billy. You'll take nothing away from anyone ever again."

"Buck," Billy said in a very calm voice, "what have I taken from you?"

"What?" Buck shouted. "You've taken everything away from Tina and me. You took my foreman job at the ranch. You took Tina's chance for success. And you ultimately took her away from me."

"I didn't even know you wanted the foreman job. I just answered an ad in the paper. I didn't even know you."

"That wouldn't have mattered. You wanted the job, and you didn't care who you stomped on to get it."

"As far as Tina's career, I didn't take it. She performed at open mic night every month, and she never won. Why do you think I'm the one who took her career away?" Billy pleaded.

Buck looked as if he thought Billy had a point, but he quickly shook his head. "Don't try to sweet talk your way out of this, you little sissy. It's not going to work."

"Buck, if you let us go, I'll do my best to help Tina's career. You know I have a record deal and the label's attention when it comes to talent. I promise you I will get Ian to help her as well." He knew this was a lie—Ian didn't want anything to do with him—but he had to save them somehow. "He used to be a talent scout, you know. And he still has connections."

"Too little, too late," Buck said. "Besides, Tina never wanted to be a star. It was all me, always pushing her. She knew she would never make it, and now I know that as well. She's no use to me anymore."

Buck picked up the first fuel can and poured gasoline all around the inside perimeter of the cabin. When the first can was empty, he poured the second can over the split-rail fence posts across the room.

Buck looked around at his handiwork. "That should send you both up in a blaze of glory in no time at all."

Tina screamed, "No! Buck, please don't do this! Please."

Billy listened to her plead with Buck to let them go, but he knew Buck had already made up his mind. Just then, Billy remembered he'd left Ian a message about Buck calling him and telling him that Jules had been hurt. If Ian got the message, he would call Jean, and they would know something wasn't right. They would come, but only if Ian listened to his message.

I've got to give Ian and Jules time to get here. I've got to stall.

Billy took a deep breath. "Buck, you know you won't get away with this."

"Says who?" Buck replied.

"We'll be missed," Billy said calmly. "Besides, where will you go after you set the cabin on fire? Ian knows you hate me, and I think Jules and Jean are on to you as well."

"Who cares about your fairy boyfriend and those other twits," Buck snarled. "By the time they find your ashes, I'll be long gone."

Buck reached into his pocket and pulled out a small box of matches.

"Wait," Billy shouted.

"What now, sissy?"

"There are people looking for us right now," Billy yelled.

"Okay, queer boy. I'll bite," Buck said. "Who's looking for you?"

"I left a message telling Ian I got a call from you and that Jules was hurt at the ranch. I know as soon as he gets that message, he's gonna call Jean, and they'll figure it all out. I'm sure they're here right now looking for us."

"Oh, really?" Buck said. "Even if you did call him, which I seriously doubt, and even if they are looking for you, they won't have any idea where to look. And besides, by the time they see the flames, you both will be toast. Say good-bye, ladies," Buck said as he struck the match and held it in front of him.

Chapter Twenty

IAN AND Todd arrived at the ranch and saw Jules and Jean running toward them. Jules had something in his hand.

Ian got out of the car and hurried to meet them, with Todd on his heels. Ian could see the stress on both of their faces, even from a distance.

"What's wrong?" Ian said. They looked at Todd. Ian said, "This is Todd. Long story, but I'll explain it all later. Now, what's wrong?"

"Okay, honey," Jean said. "We have problems."

"What do you mean?" Ian asked with a quizzical look.

"Don't panic, honey," Jean said, "but we found this baseball bat in the barn, and it's covered with blood."

Jules held the bat up for Ian and Todd to see.

Ian felt his knees about to give out. "Oh my God," he groaned as Todd and Jules caught him before he hit the ground.

Ian took a second to right himself. "I'm okay, but we need to find Billy. Now!"

"I've already called the police, and they're on their way. I don't like this at all. This is my fault," Jules said. "I knew that guy was no good. Why did I keep him around? If anything happens to Billy, I will never forgive myself."

Ian heard the wail of sirens in the distance and turned in the direction of the sound. Just over the hill, the sky was illuminated.

"What's that?" he screamed.

"Oh my heavens," Jean said.

"That's the old cabin," Jules replied.

Ian shouted Billy's name. "Jules! Billy's in that cabin, I can feel it. He's going to burn to death. We've got to get up there."

Jules told Jean to stay put and direct the police to the cabin when they arrived. Jules, Ian, and Todd jumped into Jules's truck and sped in the direction of the cabin.

When they arrived, the cabin was engulfed in flames. The walls were burning halfway up the sides, and the fire was nearing the roofline. Ian jumped out of the truck before Jules or Todd could stop him and burst through the door of the cabin. Smoke filled the small room, and Ian dropped to the floor. He began calling for Billy.

"I'm over here," Billy yelled back.

"Keep yelling so I can follow your voice," Ian shouted.

As Billy continued to call Ian's name, Ian crawled his way to the bed. Ian immediately tried to lift Billy off of the bed, but he couldn't.

"My hands and feet are tied," Billy yelled.

Ian fumbled with the rope that bound Billy's hands and soon got one free. The fire was raging, and now the roof was totally engulfed.

Ian and Billy heard Jules and Todd screaming for them. The rafters were creaking and burning and about to give way.

"Stay out of here, guys," Billy shouted. "It's too dangerous; the roof is going to give."

Ian freed Billy's other hand and moved to his feet.

Billy stopped him. "Tina. You've got to get Tina."

Ian didn't understand what Billy was talking about. Billy pointed to the other bed, and Ian saw a woman lying on it. She wasn't moving.

While Billy untied his feet, Ian started working on getting Tina free.

Jules appeared through the smoke and started to help untie Tina.

As the last rope was untied, Jules lifted Tina off the bed and headed back toward the door. Todd was there to meet him. He took Tina and carried her to safety. Billy and Ian followed, and they'd barely reached the doorjamb when the roof gave way and the cabin imploded.

Jean and the police arrived at the inflamed cabin. Jean jumped out of the squad car and ran to Jules.

"I'm fine," Jules said. "Check on the boys."

As the fire trucks were speeding up the hill, Billy and Ian helped each other away from the burning cabin to safety.

EVERYTHING WAS chaos for a while. Firefighters turned hoses on the cabin to control the flames, but the structure was a complete loss. Tina had minor burns and smoke inhalation, but the paramedics told everyone they thought she would make a full recovery just before they took her off to the hospital. Jules, Billy, and Ian all had minor burns, and Billy quite the bump on his head, but after being checked out, none of them would agree to go to the hospital. Billy told the police the full story, and they put out an all-points bulletin for Buck and assured Billy they would apprehend him before he crossed the state line.

Ian and Billy walked away from the crowd arm in arm, and Ian finally broke the silence.

"I thought I'd lost you, Billy. I love you. Can you ever forgive me?"

"I love you too, Ian," Billy said. "Can we go home now?"

"Anything you want," Ian replied. "Anything."

WHEN ALL was said and done, Jules and Jean hugged the boys and expressed their deep appreciation to Todd for his help. Although they had a clue, they still didn't know he was Ian's Todd, but as far as they were concerned, Todd was a man they could trust, and there would be time enough to get the full story later.

Todd drove Billy and Ian back to Ian's house. During the entire ride home, Ian didn't let Billy go. For the first time in eight years, he had something to lose, and he felt alive.

When they arrived, Billy went straight upstairs to shower. Ian offered Todd the guest bathroom and gave him some clean clothes. Ian went to the bedroom to shower as well and talk to Billy, but when he got to the door, Billy was sound asleep on the bed.

Ian thought how exhausted and gorgeous he looked. He grabbed some clothes, tiptoed to the bathroom, and took a long, hot shower. This was the first time he had to reflect on what had happened in the last twenty-four hours. Even he had trouble believing everything he now knew, but it was real, all of it was real.

When Ian finished showering, Billy was still asleep. Ian tiptoed out of the bedroom and went downstairs, where he found Todd sitting on the couch with a beer in his hand.

"I hope you don't mind," Todd said, "but I helped myself."

"No problem. It's the least I can do. Let me get one, and I'll join you," Ian replied.

Ian returned from the kitchen and sat on the couch next to Todd.

"What a day," Todd said.

"You're not kidding," said Ian. "I still can't believe the stuff our parents did to us. We've wasted so many years hating each other. If we had just made the effort to find one another, this could have all been cleared up."

"Do you think we didn't make the effort because we knew it wouldn't last? Was it easier to hate each other than work through the problems we would have faced if we proceeded with the relationship?" Todd asked.

"We were so young," Ian said. "I guess we'll never know the answer to that question. But I know one thing. I will never forget what you and Billy did for me and what you did for Billy."

Ian reached over and, for the first time in eight years, kissed Todd. They embraced for several minutes and said their good-byes. After Todd left Ian went back upstairs to check on Billy.

Billy was sitting on the bed with his hand over his face, wiping tears away.

"Billy! What's wrong?" Ian asked.

"I guess I knew I was taking a chance by contacting Todd, but it was a chance I was willing to take. Now that you both know the truth, will you try to work things out?"

"Why would you say that?" Ian asked.

"I woke up alone and came downstairs. I saw you and Todd embracing, and knew I had my answer."

"Why didn't you say anything?"

"I wanted to give you guys some privacy. You were both hit pretty hard with the revelations of the past, and I didn't want to come between you. I'm sure you had many things to say to one another after all these years, things that needed to be said. I thought you would need this time to sort things out, to see what was left of your relationship."

"I can't believe you did any of this," Ian said. "This is the most unselfish thing anyone has ever done for me. You took a huge risk bringing Todd and me back together."

Billy looked up, wiping his tears away with the back of his hand. "All I knew was that your story didn't add up. I put myself in Todd's place. If you loved him as much as you said you did, and I believed you did, he would have been a fool to give that up. So I tracked him down to find out the truth. Luckily my hunch proved to be right, and we soon figured out you were both duped. I know I took a risk, but if I lost you by bringing Todd here, then you were meant to be with him, not me, and I would have to live with that. At least I could go to sleep at night, knowing I did the right thing by you.

"But, Ian.... I also hoped in my heart that once you knew the truth, and if you didn't choose to go back to Todd, that maybe, just maybe, you'd want to start your life over again. With me."

Ian looked Billy in the eyes. "With you and only you. I love you, Billy."

Billy smiled with palpable relief. He stood up and pulled Ian up with him. "I love you too," Billy said as he kissed him deeply. Ian wrapped his arms around Billy and held him there for a long time.

They fell onto the bed, undressing as they went. They landed with Ian on top and Billy's arms wrapped around him tightly. Ian's mouth melted over Billy's with an urgency that neither had experienced during any of their previous lovemaking. Billy took Ian's head in his hands and pulled him back to look him the eyes. "I love you so much, Ian. Please tell me you won't give up on me, on us, again."

With his head held tightly between Billy's hands, Ian looked into Billy's eyes. "I am so in love with you, Billy. I couldn't ever give up on us. But please promise that you'll be patient with me. I've spent the last eight years teaching myself how not to love, how not to trust. It's going to take me a while to undo the damage I've done."

"You have me forever," Billy whispered.

Epilogue

THREE YEARS—and three encores—later, ten thousand people at the New Orleans Mercedes Super Dome were on their feet and begging for more of hometown boy and country superstar Billy Eagan. With hat in hand, he took one last bow, waved, and turned to exit. As he walked the span of the long stage, he thought about how much he loved the way performing made him feel. The energy, the love, the acceptance. But all those things, he understood, were for the person his record label and the media had portrayed him to be, not for him. Would his fans ever get to know the real Billy Eagan, the way in which he lived his personal life or the man with which he passionately shared it? That Billy Eagan they'd probably never know.

FROM THE wings, Ian admired the man he loved, cherished, and protected. He watched as Billy went through his final bows, turned, and began to walk toward him. Billy was rapidly approaching with what Ian recognized all too well as the same adrenaline rush he experienced after every show. He seemed to be floating on air. As if seeing Billy for the first time, Ian was again reminded of just how strikingly handsome he was.

Ian was snapped out of his daydream when Billy put his left hand on his shoulder and squeezed three times. Ian instantly knew the sign. It was something they'd developed as a discreet way to say "I love you" when they were in the watchful eye of the public.

They exchanged a glance of mutual admiration before Ian handed Billy a towel and a bottle of water.

With the crowd still roaring for more, his band played an instrumental version of Billy's latest single and waited for a sign from Ian as to whether another encore was in order. Billy asked, "Should I go out one more time?"

"Are you crazy?" Ian laughed. "Three encores is more than enough on top of a two-and-a-half-hour show."

"I know, I know," Billy said sheepishly. "But it's not easy to know when enough is enough. I certainly don't want to disappoint these guys."

"Hell, Billy, this is opening night," Ian said. "You've got to pace yourself. You're about to do five sold-out shows a week for the next ten months. And in a dozen of those cities, you've already convinced the label to add a second show to make sure everyone gets in.

"Look, I understand how you feel about performing. I know the dedication and love you feel for the people who support you. And I know after me, performing is your lifeline, but you've got to be realistic, Billy. You can't kill yourself in the first week."

Billy smiled. "You're right, Ian. You're always right."

Ian signaled the band that they were through. They gave a big finish, and within seconds, the stage lights were out, the house lights were up, and people were finally exiting their seats.

"How did I get so lucky?" Billy asked.

"You won't think you're so lucky when I tell you about tomorrow's schedule," Ian replied.

"I'll be the judge of that. Give it to me straight," Billy said.

"Okay, you're on *Good Morning America*, via the local ABC affiliate, tomorrow morning at seven thirty. At eight forty-five, you're being interviewed on the morning show at WNOE radio, and immediately following that, a photo shoot for the cover of *New Orleans* magazine. We have a twelve thirty flight tomorrow afternoon, which puts us in Atlanta by two o'clock and will give us a few hours of downtime before sound checks and the meet and greet preceding the show. The crew and the band, on the other hand, are packing and loading the equipment now and will be leaving tonight, and should make it to Phillips Arena by 8:00 a.m."

"I'm still lucky," Billy said as they walked back to his dressing room with Ian's arm draped across Billy's shoulders, in a very managerial way, laughing and recounting stories about the night's performance. Once inside, Billy sat on the couch with his feet up and watched as Ian, on his cell phone, finalized more details for the next show. He realized he had everything he ever wanted. His career would someday fade away, but if he had Ian, he needed nothing more. They had overcome so much to get here, and they were never looking back.

Coming Soon!

After the Final Encore

Encore: Book Three

By Scotty Cade

Country superstar Billy Eagan's career is soaring. He's topping the charts and winning award after award. He and his manager and life partner Ian Dillon have been virtually inseparable for almost five years, solidifying their relationship as well as Billy's skyrocketing stardom. After a secret kiss between the two of them at an awards show is caught on camera, a tabloid newspaper outs Billy and Ian as lovers, which could sabotage Billy's career on the bigoted Nashville music scene. To make matter worse, an old adversary rears his ugly head and threatens to end everything Billy and Ian have worked for—including their lives.

http://www.dreamspinnerpress.com

Don't miss how the
story started!

Before the Final Encore

Encore: Book One

By Scotty Cade

Tires flying over the interstate, college student Ian Dillon can't get out of Greenville, SC quickly enough. As he watches his entire life fading away in his rearview mirror, his thoughts are only of his lover, Todd, and the memories of their time together, now completely shattered by Todd's incomprehensible betrayal. His mind still reeling, Ian drives through the night until a split second decision guides him to Nashville, Tennessee. Everything will be better there. It has to be!

http://www.dreamspinnerpress.com

SCOTTY CADE left Corporate America and twenty-five years of marketing and public relations in 2004 to buy an inn & restaurant on the island of Martha's Vineyard with his husband of nearly twenty years.

He started writing stories as soon as he could read, but only recently for publication. When not at the inn, you can find him on the bow of his boat writing romance novels with his Shetland sheepdog Mavis at his side. Being from the South and a lover of commitment and fidelity, most of his characters find their way to long, healthy relationships, however long it takes them to get there. He believes that, in the end, the boy should always get the boy.

Scotty and his partner are avid boaters and live aboard their boat, spending the summers on Martha's Vineyard and winters in various locations down south.

Visit Scotty at http://www.scottycade.com and Scotty Cade on Facebook @scotty.cade.com and on Twitter @ScottyCade. You can also contact him at scotty@scottycade.com.

Acting Out

By Scotty Cade

After one very long tour of duty in Afghanistan and an honorable discharge from the USMC, Elijah Preston comes home to nothing. He barely scrapes up enough money for a cheap motel in Quantico, Virginia, with no money-making opportunities in sight. A chance encounter in a local Walmart finally gives Eli hope for employment. Elijah is ready to sign on with Royce Mackey's proposition... until he hears what's required. Royce operates a gay military porn site and wants Eli as his next star, never mind that Eli isn't gay. Desperate and broke, Eli grudgingly accepts Royce's offer and soon finds himself immersed in a strange new world.

Hamish Turner's been there before. Taking Eli under his wing, he teaches him everything he can about Royce's operation. The two quickly become friends, easing the way for their first scene together. Awkward at first, they both ease into it and find there is more of a connection between them than either expected. Curious to see where their mutual attraction takes them, they begin a relationship off-screen. But life gets complicated when a crazed fan of Hamish's starts sending threatening letters demanding the scenes between the two men stop. Or else….

http://www.dreamspinnerpress.com

The Mystery of Ruby Lode

By Scotty Cade

After six months of research, adventure seekers Bowen McAlister, Cyrus Curran, Duff Gentry, and Lockhart Dawson make their way to Boulder, Colorado, to explore the abandoned gold mine Ruby Lode. But when they arrive, Duff, a born psychic, senses something isn't quite right—and the closer they get, the more his unease grows.

Something long buried in the deep shafts and drifts of Ruby Lode makes its presence known by exposing dark, guarded secrets. Preying on the adventurers' weaknesses and insecurities, Ruby Lode's own destructive secret threatens their sanity, friendship, and ultimately their lives. Bo, Cy, Duff, and Lockey must work together to unravel the century-old mystery before they become another footnote in the mine's history.

http://www.dreamspinnerpress.com

The Royal Street Heist

By Scotty Cade

When valuable Civil War era art is stolen from a popular New Orleans gallery, NOPD Lead Detective Montgomery "Beau" Bissonet and his partner set out to solve the crime. When the gallery's insurance company sends Tollison Cruz to the Big Easy to conduct their own independent investigation, personalities clash and battle lines are definitely drawn.

The heist quickly becomes a politically driven high profile case, and Detective Bissonet is furious when he's ordered to work alongside Investigator Cruz to assure a timely arrest. The heat index soars to new levels when the two investigators discover they have a lot more in common than originally thought.

With the tension between them temporarily sated, Bissonet and Cruz finally start to work together, on more than just a professional level. But everything comes to a screeching halt when Beau discovers his cohort in crime has been withholding information regarding the investigation and has been concealing a very questionable past. What happens next rivals the scorching summer heat.

http://www.dreamspinnerpress.com

Sunrise Over Savannah

By Scotty Cade

Thompson and Caroline Gray were living their dream until Caroline's untimely death just two years after they'd bought the Thundercloud Marina. When Caroline died, she left Thompson alone and emotionally disconnected—until Thompson's longtime friend and towboat owner Hank Charming tows Garner Holt, a recently retired psychiatrist, and his boat into the marina for repair. Thompson and Hank are both drawn to the sailboat captain, but for very different reasons.

Since high school, Hank has secretly carried a torch for Thompson, even though Thompson remained committed to Caroline, even after her death. Hank is totally caught off guard when his initial attraction to Garner makes him realize this stranger might be the one to help him move on with his life. Thompson establishes a platonic friendship with Garner and starts to see the psychiatrist as his only lifeline to sanity. Life improves until Thompson sees Hank and Garner together, and old feelings Thompson thought were long buried begin to resurface. Garner quickly identifies the unresolved feelings between Hank and Thompson and decides to tap his professional skills and work behind the scenes to help Thompson and Hank see what has been right in front of them all along.

http://www.dreamspinnerpress.com

Chasing the Horizon

By Scotty Cade

Needing a lifestyle change, Garner Holt, an uptight workaholic psychologist, buys a sailboat and trades in his prestigious job in New York City for a life on the water. After engine failure and six weeks in Savannah, Georgia for repair, he arrives in Key West, Florida early one morning and encounters a half-dressed hooligan walking along the docks of the marina. Garner immediately thinks this barefoot and shirtless man with a shaved head, multiple tattoos, and piercings in every orifice is going to rob him. He prepares for the worst. Instead, the stranger passes Garner by and climbs on a boat a few slips down. With the threat of danger gone, Garner is surprisingly intrigued.

Hawken Bristol is used to being on the receiving end of stereotypes. He sees the fear on the stranger's face, recognizes the rigidity in his stance, but is too tired from his wild night of partying to engage the frightened stranger. A few cat and mouse encounters around town lead to an uncanny attraction. However, after Garner helps Hawken dock his boat in a windstorm, sparks start to fly. But this new liaison brings up old baggage that threatens to derail everything they have going.

http://www.dreamspinnerpress.com

An Unconventional Courtship

By Scotty Cade

Tristan Moreau loves his job as chief administrative officer and personal assistant to Webber Kincaid, President, Chairman, and CEO of Kincaid International. It would be the perfect job… if only he hadn't fallen in love with his boss as well as the work. After two years, he's still doing everything in his power to keep his feelings hidden—mostly because he wants to protect the reputation of his famous boss but also because he wants to keep his job.

Webber Kincaid has stayed in the closet, using his best friend and confidante as his beard. Everything in his life was working out just fine until he met Tristan Moreau. Within months, Tristan stole his heart and became his lifeline. But Webber knows the rules of the workplace better than anyone, so he's kept his distance.

But two years is too long to wonder "what if?"—especially when business takes them to a private Caribbean island. When Tristan and Webber succumb to the tropical heat, their professionalism starts to backslide. It's a seemingly impossible relationship, making a go at it under the paparazzi's microscope. It may be the best—or the worst—business decision they ever made.

An Unconventional Union

By Scotty Cade

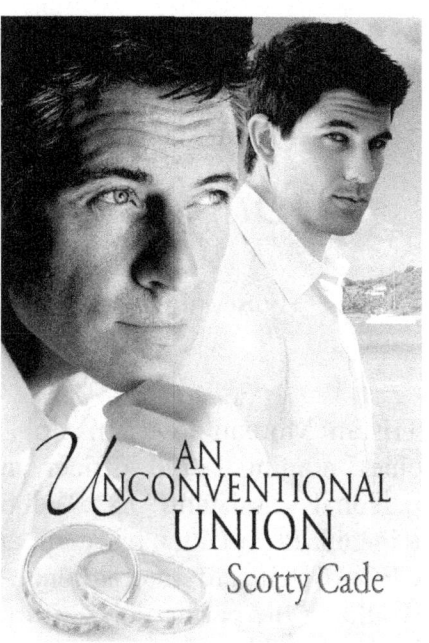

Kincaid International Corporation's CEO, Webber Kincaid, and his executive assistant, Tristan Moreau, have just returned from a Caribbean business trip gone horribly right. After years of hiding their love for each other, they finally came clean—and discovered KIC's chief financial officer has been up to some shady business transactions. Now that they're back, Tristan and Webber must expose the CFO's indiscretions—and save Webber's reputation, since he's ultimately responsible for his CFO's actions. With Tristan by his side, Webber faces KIC's board of directors and a looming investigation by the Securities and Exchange Commission and Department of Justice.

With all the uncertainty surrounding them, Webber and Tristan rely on the strength of their connection. Together, they plan an intimate wedding on the island of Martha's Vineyard. But despite their love for one another, Webber and Tristan quickly realize they have some hurdles to cross before they can start their unexpected new life.

http://www.dreamspinnerpress.com

Wings of Love

Love Series

By Scotty Cade

Devastated after losing his partner of fifteen years to cancer, Dr. Bradford Mitchell tries to escape the emptiness and loss by leaving his life in Seattle behind. Traveling to the Alaskan mountains where he and Jeff often vacationed, Brad reconnects with Mac Cleary, the ruggedly handsome and very straight floatplane pilot who had flown them to Hyline Lake many times in the past. Brad and Mac form an unlikely friendship and buy an old log cabin together, and as he and Mac begin to bring the old cabin back to life, Mac watches Brad come back to life as well, stirring emotions in him he's never felt for a man before.

When fear, confusion, and a near tragedy threaten to force the two men apart, they'll face some tough questions. Can Brad let go of Jeff and the guilt he feels about beginning to care for another man? And can Mac deal with his fears of being gay and accept the fact that he is in love with Brad? It will be a struggle for both men to keep their heads and hearts intact while exploring what life has to offer.

http://www.dreamspinnerpress.com

Bounty of Love

Love Series

By Scotty Cade

The night before his wedding, Zander Walsh, his parents, and his husband-to-be are all shot when they return home and interrupt a mysterious robbery in progress. After three weeks in a coma, Zander wakes up to find out he is the only survivor, and his perfect life falls apart in an instant.

Hunky FBI Agent Jake Elliot is investigating the case, and he eventually apprehends the killer—who soon escapes. Following six months of searching, Zander and Jake realize they're being stonewalled by the FBI... and that they have slowly formed an unbreakable bond that is beginning to turn into much more.

Once they embark on a journey to apprehend the killer for the second time, they'll discover that one terrible night was much more than just an interrupted robbery. Can big business and politics cover up the truth, or will Zander and Jake's quest to unravel the mystery be the end of their newfound love and their lives?

http://www.dreamspinnerpress.com

Treasure of Love

Love Series

By Scotty Cade

Hunky Alaskan dive master and charter boat captain Jackson Cameron is absolutely sure he's straight until openly gay treasure hunter Dax Powers calls him and offers him the adventure of a lifetime: Dax and his sister Donatella have found the Anna Wyoming, a ship that went down during the 1889 gold rush on return from Skagway Island—very possibly carrying a fortune in gold.

But real treasure is never free, and this one comes with some heavily armed strings attached. Jack and Dax struggle to keep their small crew safe from a powerful threat while they fight against the attraction they feel for each other. Between the danger of the hunt, the risks in the dive, and the thrill of being lost in passion, Dax and Jack are going to have a hard time holding on to their treasure... and to each other!

http://www.dreamspinnerpress.com

Foundation of Love

Love Series

By Scotty Cade & Z.B. Marshall

Years ago, Wes Stanhope fled his hometown of Charleston to escape the constraints of society and his controlling father, Colonel Robert Lee Stanhope IV. After completing medical school and building a successful practice in pediatric oncology in Seattle, Wes is called home for his mother's funeral and presented with an opportunity to build and run a children's hospital—his mother's legacy—a choice he ultimately makes despite his misgivings about his father's role as chairman of the hospital's board of directors.

When Wes begins to build his team, he is introduced to a young, handsome black architect named Tyler Williams. Sparks begin to fly between the two men, and although Wes doesn't identify as gay, denying his attraction to Ty becomes impossible. But Ty won't be a dirty secret: if Wes wants to build a relationship, he'll have to come out, brave his father's racism and homophobia, and risk his chance to continue as the hospital's CEO and realize his mother's dream.

http://www.dreamspinnerpress.com

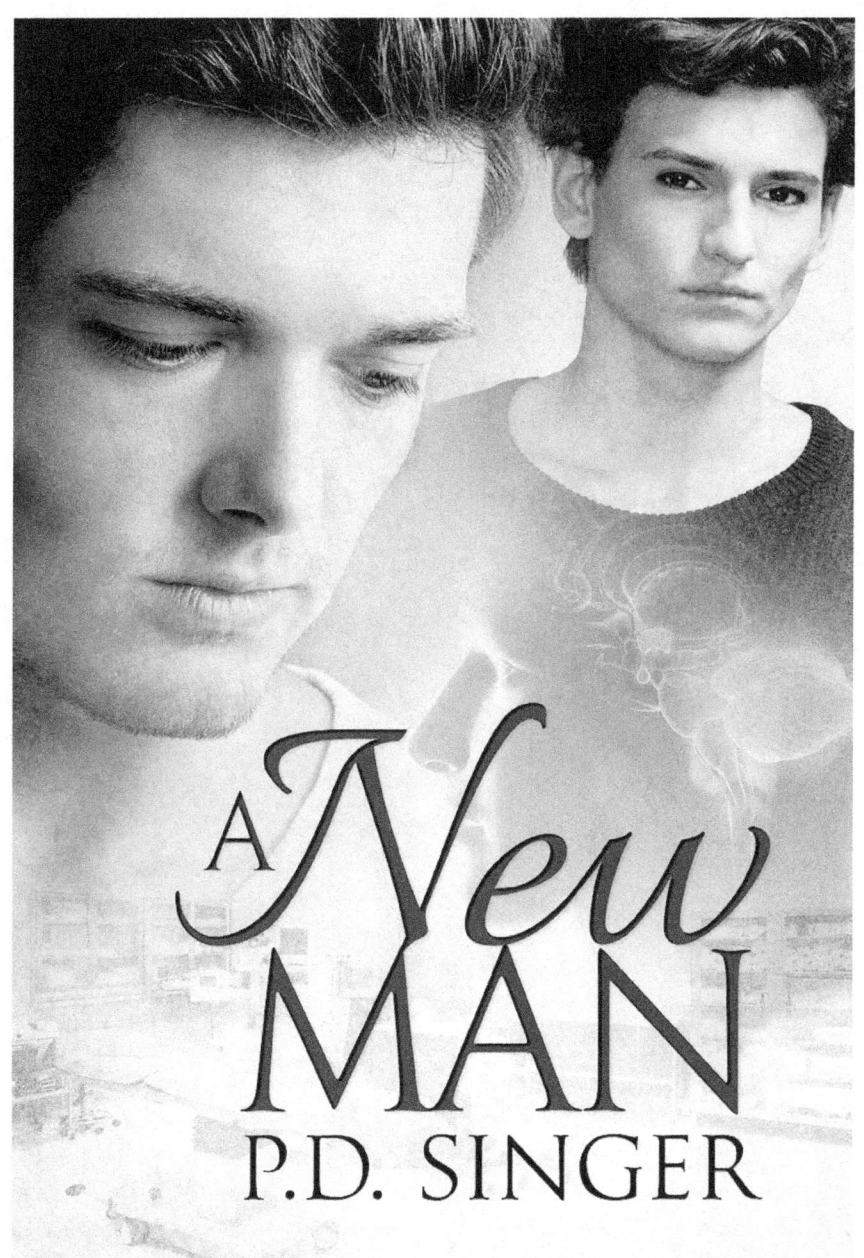

A New

MAN

P.D. SINGER

http://www.dreamspinnerpress.com

JACOB Z. FLORES

Please
REMEMBER
Me

http://www.dreamspinnerpress.com

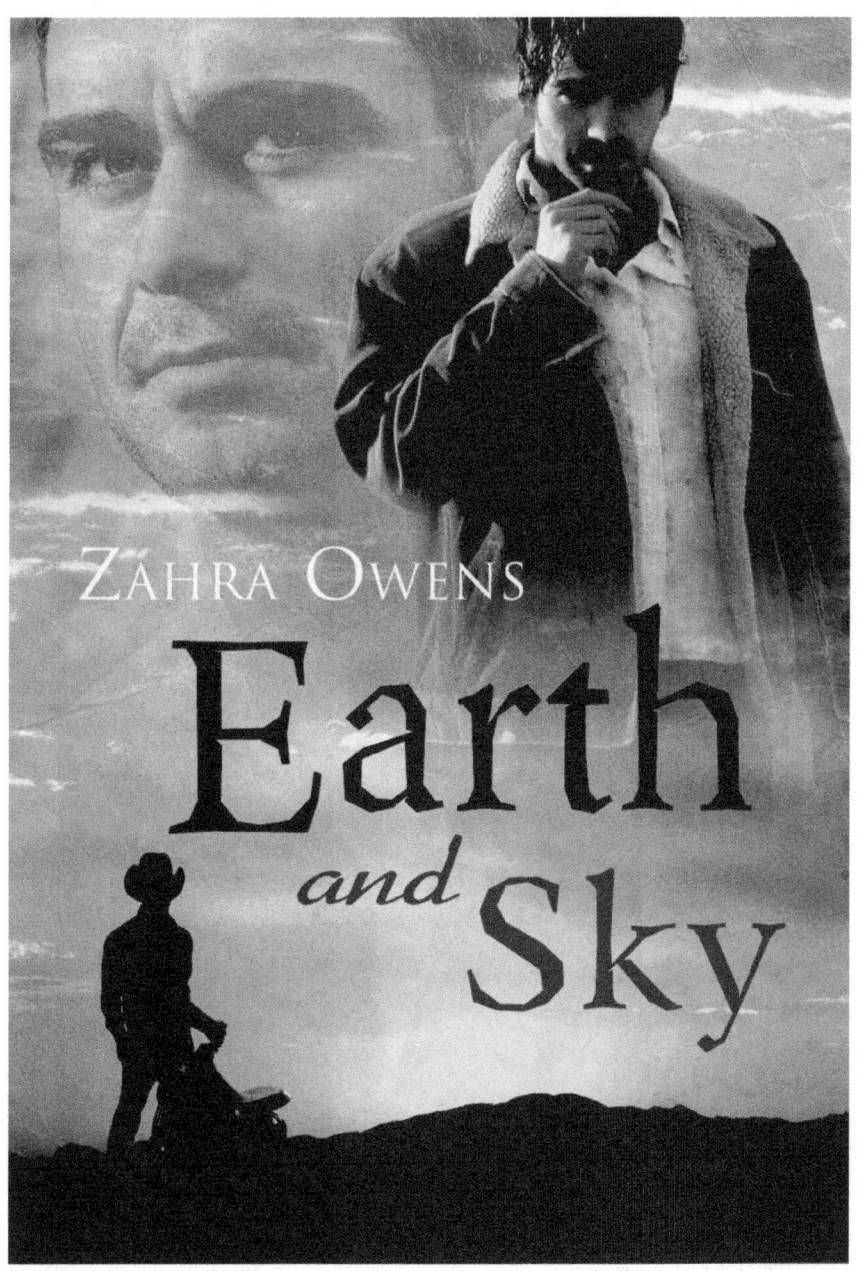

ZAHRA OWENS

Earth
and Sky

http://www.dreamspinnerpress.com

FOR **MORE** OF THE **BEST GAY** ROMANCE

Made in United States
Orlando, FL
22 March 2026

79559121R00118